"If you think I'm going to let my fiancé run off with some stupid American maid," Lavinia said, *"then you've got another thing coming, Max!"*

Max felt the hopelessness of his cause, felt Elizabeth slipping farther and farther away. "But Lavinia, I don't love you. You don't even love me."

Lavinia didn't seem to be listening. She'd already turned her attention back toward her voluminous closets. "What?" she asked distractedly, holding up a navy dress and a black dress against her body and checking her reflection critically in the full-length mirror. "Oh, Max, do stop being so tedious and hand me that comb, will you?"

Max looked to his left at the tortoiseshell comb and then back at Lavinia. He didn't make a move. It was time to bring out the big guns. "Lavinia, I don't want to marry you," he said flatly.

This brought Lavinia's maneuvers to a halt. She turned to Max, threw both dresses on the bed, and came to stand in front of him. He could smell the harsh, too-sweet perfume that clung to all of her clothing.

"Max," Lavinia said icily. "The invitations have been sent. The gifts have been received. Princess *Stephanie* has _____ come. And you will be *standing* with _____ hether you like it or _____

Bantam Books in the Elizabeth series.
Ask your bookseller for the books you have missed.

Visit the Official Sweet Valley Web Site on the Internet at:
www.sweetvalley.com

Elizabeth

I Need You

WRITTEN BY
LAURIE JOHN

CREATED BY
FRANCINE PASCAL

BANTAM BOOKS
NEW YORK • TORONTO • LONDON • SYDNEY • AUCKLAND

RL: 8, AGES 14 AND UP

I NEED YOU
A Bantam Book / June 2001

*Produced by 17th Street Productions,
an Alloy Online, Inc. company.
33 West 17th Street
New York, NY 10011.*

ISBN: 0-553-49358-2

Visit us on the Web! www.randomhouse.com/teens

Published simultaneously in the United States and Canada

Bantam Books is an imprint of Random House Children's Books, a division
of Random House, Inc. BANTAM BOOKS and the rooster colophon are
registered trademarks of Random House, Inc. Bantam Books, 1540
Broadway, New York, New York 10036.

PRINTED IN THE UNITED STATES OF AMERICA

OPM   0 9 8 7 6 5 4 3 2 1

To Mia Pascal Johansson

Chapter
One

"Quite a view," Elizabeth Wakefield murmured, holding both hands tightly around the mug of hot coffee she'd brought outside into the freezing cold of the English countryside.

Her breath came out in a thick plume as she regarded the stunning, rolling grounds of Pennington House, which had been covered for the past couple of weeks or so under a spotless blanket of white snow. Shifting from one foot to the other to keep warm, Elizabeth took a sip of her still scalding coffee and let her gaze travel nonchalantly up the ivy-strung front of the house toward Max Pennington's window. She wondered if he was in his room, snuggled in bed . . . the bed that they had—

A delivery truck slowly wound its way up the snow-covered back drive, and Elizabeth was grateful for the distraction. Ever since December 1,

Pennington House could have doubled as a post office with all of the deliveries and pickups that had rolled up and down the gravel driveway—all coordinated and received by the household help, of course, who had been mobilized into a wedding-planning corps.

I can't believe I'm actually waiting for another five-hundred-dollar piece of crystal to be delivered to Max and his wife-to-be, Elizabeth thought, trying to push down the panicky, overstuffed feeling that took over her chest every time she pictured herself in bed with Max.

Leave it to me to protect my virginity and save it for that really special someone, then finally give it away to a guy who's getting married in a matter of weeks, she thought sadly. *At a wedding where— might I add—I'll be refilling champagne flutes and running around to get barons and earls ashtrays for their stinky cigars.*

Elizabeth swallowed hard and stamped her feet on the granite steps. She'd been swallowing hard for the past month, but right now, she didn't know what else to do. So she avoided looking at Max's window and watched the truck inch its way up the curving drive.

It had all started six months ago in June, back on that first night when she'd been serving the Pennington family, really—when Elizabeth had ignored the advice of the other maid, Vanessa, to keep her face blank and remember her place with her *employers*. Instead she had allowed herself to fall headfirst for gorgeous, grinning, brown-haired Max, sitting at the dinner table—and refused to acknowledge that titles and seats in Parliament meant a lot more than some old episode of *Fawlty Towers* would lead you to believe. She'd bantered with him, joked across the tablecloth with him, worked hard to impress him night after night—that is, whenever his father, the earl, didn't interrupt with a smooth, *That will be all, Elizabeth*.

But there hadn't been only eye contact and flirting. Many times they'd sought each other out in the gardens of Pennington House: first, to talk about writing and literature, which both of them loved, and later to discuss family problems and how much responsibility you really had toward your family. That was a subject Elizabeth herself wasn't too clear on right now but was only too happy to discuss with someone equally as confused as she was.

But of course, things had snowballed in exactly the way Elizabeth had both wished for and feared. They—well, *she*, at least—had fallen in love. And the night that Max had told her that Lavinia was blackmailing him into marrying her, Elizabeth had thrown away all of her caution and acted on it. *I couldn't have stopped myself if I'd tried*, Elizabeth thought, remembering. She bit her lip and blushed, a wave of heat rising through her entire body at the thought of Max's strong shoulders, the tangled sheets. She had to take deep breaths and shake her head quickly to clear it.

And suddenly, she wasn't shivering anymore.

With a start Elizabeth jerked out of her reverie. The truck was slowly pulling to a stop. The crystalware for the place settings, no doubt. Or the tables themselves. Or another unbelievably lavish gift—a harpsichord and pair of Louis VI wing-backed chairs were among the gifts that had already been received and logged and were now languishing in a wing devoted to that purpose—for the happy couple.

With a jerk Elizabeth tossed her now cold coffee out on the lawn. It left a stain like a wound in the foot-deep powder. She shoved the mug in her parka pocket and plastered a fake, efficient smile on her face for the deliveryman, who had pulled up and was descending from the truck's cab.

"Morning," Elizabeth called.

A strange image arose. Elizabeth found herself suddenly wishing with all her heart that she was back in Sweet Valley, sitting at Yum-Yums with her best friend, Nina, tearing into the Sunday brunch of scrambled eggs and hash browns with the rest of the junior class. The sense of loss was momentarily

4

so powerful that Elizabeth could feel it, almost like a blow to the solar plexus.

Her sudden affection for the Sweet Valley of old took Elizabeth completely by surprise—up until now, she had only been able to associate Sweet Valley with her sister and her ex-boyfriend kissing in a motel room and the dry taste of betrayal in her mouth when she had opened the flimsy door and discovered them all over each other in the hallway. But for now she was in Yum-Yums again, and it seemed unbearably sweet. She could smell the bacon cooking, hear the lazy chatter of her classmates, see the surfboards propped up by the tables of optimistic diners who were going to hit the surf before the day was out. Wishing she could just reach over and pull out a seat for herself, she inhaled the memory.

I guess it's natural that I'd be missing Sweet Valley, Elizabeth thought. *It is only a week before Christmas, after all.*

Elizabeth blinked back tears. She was standing in the cold out front at Pennington House, one arm dangling in front of her like she was waking the dead, waiting to log in gifts for her ex-lover.

"Miss," said the driver, a cap pulled down over his lined and weathered features. Elizabeth realized that he had probably been trying to get her attention for quite some time. He tapped his pen against his dull gray clipboard. "I'll be needin' your signature right here for delivery."

Elizabeth jerked her hand back to her side. "Sorry!" she exclaimed, leaping for the pen and scribbling her name—well, the phony name she was known as in England, Elizabeth Bennet—on the line the driver pointed to with one ink-stained finger. "I've been standing out in the cold too long, I guess."

"You're American!" said the driver, pointing the pen with gleeful abandon as he heard the unfamiliar cadences of Elizabeth's voice. "I guess that explains it well enough."

Elizabeth smiled—a real one, this time. "Just pull the truck around to the loading area in the back," she said with as much dignity as she could muster. "Some of the staff should be there to help you."

As the small truck chugged off, Elizabeth turned on her heel, prepared to open the heavy front door and return to the blessed heat of Pennington House. But as her fingers touched the doorknob, a car door slamming and a shout stopped her. "Elizabeth!" she heard. Suddenly Max was at her side.

Elizabeth felt as tongue-tied as she had been those early days in their relationship—no, twice as tongue-tied. "Hi," she managed, knowing that if she said any more, she'd either burst into tears, punch Max on the arm, or knock him flat against the door with a passionate kiss.

"Hi," Max said, looking into her eyes for a moment. He pulled open the door and gestured for her to enter first.

Elizabeth readied herself to depart with an air of aggrieved industry, the mask her coworker Vanessa Shaw always successfully assumed to get her out of sticky situations with those pesky people, her employers. Ever since she and Max had slept together, in fact, Elizabeth had employed a series of similar ruses to keep herself from being alone with him. And it had been working. It had been working so well, in fact, that Elizabeth had come to suspect that Max was also making a similar effort to deprive himself of his previously hardwon face time with *her*.

I guess he really meant it when he said we'd always have the "memory" of each other, Elizabeth thought with a small shudder, hating the fact that she was standing so close to Max and loving every second of it at the same time.

"Will you two snowbirds stop letting all the heat out?" Vanessa's menacingly sweet contralto trilled through the foyer, which she was dutifully waxing by hand, kneeling with her hands on her hips, a scrub brush in her hand and a can of wax at her side. "That's if you can stand to tear yourself away from the mistletoe," she added grumpily, leaning back over the already shining tiles.

To her left, Elizabeth could hear Max sharply inhale. *Oh, no,* she thought. They looked up at the same time. A frond of mistletoe looked back, seeming to wink enticingly.

Bull's-eye.

For the first time in weeks Elizabeth returned Max's gaze head-on, without flinching. His eyebrow was lifted in a typical expression of doubt. Her face burning with shame, Elizabeth was about to pull back and disappear into the kitchen or whatever other convenient hole she could find when Max suddenly murmured, "Shall we?" and took her firmly in his arms.

The kiss was like an emotional water balloon—all of her resistance shattered. *I know this is stupid,* Elizabeth thought as all her senses rushed forward like a fire licking at her lips, chest, knees, and belly: all the parts that were pulled firmly against Max. *But so help me, I'm not going to stop him, even if Vanessa starts beating me with that wax brush.*

Vanessa, however—Elizabeth saw when Max finally pulled away—was too rigid with shock to do anything of the kind. Max looked slowly from Vanessa to Elizabeth, his eyes looking more like those of a deer caught in the headlights every second. "Beg—beg pardon, Elizabeth," Max finally stammered, holding her so tightly with the tips of his fingers that her arms still ached later that night. Then with one last quick, frightened glance back at Elizabeth, he practically shoved her away and disappeared up the steps like her face had suddenly become that of a drooling corpse.

Elizabeth regained her balance. Looking at Vanessa, she tried to hide her grief in a faltering smile, but her sudden sense of despair was too overwhelming. *I mean, that was like a kamikaze attack,* she tried to rationalize. *He totally took me by surprise.* But it was no good. She burst into tears, weeping jerkily like a CD with a deep scratch.

Her face in her hands, Elizabeth was surprised to feel the cool pressure of Vanessa's arms around her shoulders and hear Vanessa's voice in her ear.

"You're coming upstairs to our room and telling me every detail this minute," Vanessa ordered.

Eighteen-year-old Vanessa Shaw hadn't realized how much affection she'd gained for the American maid until she saw her and Max, like some heinous *tableau vivant,* act out precisely the scene that her mother and the earl must have gone through nearly two decades ago.

She had been minding her own business, doing some work for once to keep her superirritating boss, Mary Dale, off the warpath. (Since the wedding preparations had gone into full swing, living and working in Pennington House had come to resemble military maneuvers, with that human ice sculpture of a bride-to-be, Lavinia Thurston, leading the charge.) But suddenly Max and Elizabeth had burst in from the outside. Vanessa *had* pointed out the mistletoe, but it was only to get them to shut the bloody door, which was letting in an icy wind, as well as snow, across her freshly cleaned floor.

Bloody hell. Did that mean this was all her fault?

Then Max and Elizabeth had gone into what seemed like almost a cruel parody of the disaster that Vanessa had warned Elizabeth was going to happen if she kept flirting with the son of the house. Max had swept Elizabeth into his arms like he was auditioning for Bogie's role in *Casablanca* or something. Elizabeth had gone limp in his arms, but that wasn't the worst of it. Max had finished his kiss, then dispatched her like year-old milk. Typical.

And he had ruined her nice clean floor!

Watching Elizabeth burst into a sudden storm of tears, Vanessa's habitual rage had raised its seething head, moving so quickly that she could almost hear the blood roaring in her ears. But a new, slightly uncomfortable feeling had also arisen, prickling the hairs on the back of Vanessa's head.

Vanessa felt *protective*.

Before she knew it, she had practically carried Elizabeth up the three flights of stairs and arranged her like an infant on her own cot under the window, making sure her hands and feet were covered. She went to the bathroom, filled a glass of water, and placed it at Elizabeth's side. At the last minute she grabbed a box of tissues out of their other roommate's trunk and held them in her lap at the ready.

"Now. What happened?" Vanessa finally asked.

If Vanessa felt uncomfortable with her new mothering instinct, Elizabeth looked too bombed out to even notice her new and improved attitude. *Why, the girl's totally destroyed!* Vanessa thought, taking in Elizabeth's listless expression, darkened, vacant eyes, and the silent tears that continued to roll down. *Thank God I'm going to blow this family to bits. They deserve everything that's coming to them!*

As Vanessa leaned forward to hand Elizabeth a tissue, Elizabeth's breath caught, and she jerked with another sob. "I'm just—just—so stupid," she finally gasped.

"You're not stupid," Vanessa said automatically. It occurred to her that she was now having one of those guys-are-bastards conversations you heard all the time between various weeping women in magazines and on the telly. Well, it wasn't like she hadn't had the same one millions of times with her mum before she passed away.

Elizabeth looked at Vanessa balefully. "I *am* stupid," she said. "You told me exactly what was going to happen, and now it's happened."

Vanessa tried to be gentle—a little easier, in her new Nurse Betty phase. "What happened?" she asked carefully.

Elizabeth took a deep breath, crumpling and recrumpling the tissue Vanessa had placed in her lap. Blowing her nose furiously, she hurled the tissue across the room and leaned back, closing her eyes. "Max and I, um, had . . . an affair," she said.

Vanessa gasped despite herself. People were amazing. In her wildest dreams, she'd never thought that the innocent American and the spoiled pretty boy could ever have gone that far.

"You had sex?" Vanessa burst out, then instantly regretted it. "Not—not that there's anything wrong with that," she stammered.

Elizabeth took another deep breath and shook her head. She swung both legs over the side of the bed and sat up. "Once. Just one time."

Well, now doesn't that just sound familiar? Vanessa thought, thinking of the earl downstairs in his study, happily chewing on his pipe or whatever

12

it was he did when he wasn't deflowering young maids like her mum.

"And of course there's something *wrong* with it, Vanessa," Elizabeth said, giving her what Vanessa was happy to see was almost a sly smile. "He is about to get married, you know."

Vanessa raised an eyebrow, thinking of the endless evenings she and Elizabeth had spent recently logging gifts and helping handymen arrange annoying perfect parallel rows of holly and silver bells. "Oh, he is? I hadn't noticed."

After a beat she and Elizabeth both burst into giggles. "Well, I really am stupid if I can laugh," Elizabeth finally said, reaching for another tissue and blowing her nose. "At a time like this, I mean."

But Vanessa wasn't ready to give up on the story yet. "Elizabeth," she probed, hoping that she wasn't going to send the maid off on another round of sobs. "How did it happen?"

But Elizabeth was dry-eyed—clearly, Vanessa was realizing, she was made of stronger stuff than Vanessa had given her credit for. "It's a long story," Elizabeth warned.

Vanessa lay down on Elizabeth's cot and threw her hands into the air. "It's not like we're having a wedding in a week or anything," she crowed. "We've got all the time in the world!" Elizabeth blanched. "Sorry," Vanessa said again. She wasn't doing well with her jokes today.

"I just want to wash my face," Elizabeth said, slipping out of the room. When she returned, she looked more like her old self—blond hair pulled back in a tight ponytail, skin glowing. Only the tiniest bit of red around her blue-green eyes and perfect nose, Vanessa thought, betrayed the fact that minutes ago she had been crying like it was the end of *Titanic.*

"It's not really that long a story," Elizabeth said, sitting down on the bed with a grimace. "And you saw most of it."

"You mean the kiss?" Vanessa asked, confused. She *had* been distracted by the waxing of the floor, but not so distracted that Max and Elizabeth could have consummated their affair right in front of her.

"No, I mean all those dinners and talks in the garden," Elizabeth continued. Vanessa shook her head and clucked sympathetically. God, where was all this stuff coming from? "You were right. We—we fell in love. At least *I* did," Elizabeth burst out, tears suddenly threatening to spill over again.

Vanessa leaped forward with the tissue box, but Elizabeth waved her away, holding her breath and staying still until the tears receded.

"When he told me he loved me that night,"

14

Elizabeth went on, "I just cracked. We both thought that it would be better to have one night if we couldn't have the rest of our lives."

Vanessa tried to look sympathetic again, although this time she thought that Elizabeth sounded positively dotty.

"Now every time we see each other, it's like *that*," Elizabeth continued bitterly. "It's got to stop."

"Yes, you've got to put a stop to it," Vanessa agreed hastily. This was a philosophy she could understand—cut and run, before the blokes took you for everything you had. "Cut him off, with no funny business."

Vanessa knew exactly how Elizabeth would respond. "That would be easier," Elizabeth said, "if I wasn't still completely in love with him."

Vanessa handed Elizabeth another tissue—that confession had prompted still more tears.

"Well," Vanessa said, sitting up briskly, "you're well rid of him." Her own voice echoed silently like some ancient gong. She shivered. That had been her mother's words running through her head for a minute there—not her own.

Elizabeth smiled faintly. "I just wish I could believe that," she said.

But Vanessa wasn't even talking to Elizabeth anymore.

"You're well rid of him," she repeated. "We all are, you know. We're well rid of the *lot* of them."

Twenty-one-year-old Max Pennington hurled his coat against the wall and sank down on the bed. "Damn!" he said through gritted teeth. "Damn, damn, damn, damn, damn, damn, damn!"

This was getting ridiculous. First, he had taken Elizabeth's virginity in his own bedroom—*Like the worst guy there ever was,* Max thought. And *now* he was kissing her passionately, in *full view* of the entire household, jeopardizing not only her job and her mental health, but the silence of his seething fiancée, Lavinia, who might blow any minute and flatten his family like Mount Vesuvius with her terrible secret.

What was he thinking?

Listen, mate, Max railed at himself. *First of all, leave Elizabeth alone. Don't you worry about how your actions affect her? Fine, you're so dizzy with love that you want to slip an engagement ring on her finger and run off to Switzerland every time you see her. But Lavinia's put a stop to that, and you know you can't sacrifice your family just to get the girl of your dreams. So suck it up! And stop torturing her!*

Grimacing like someone was turning a screwdriver around in his brain, Max began to slowly and methodically beat his head against the wall. It was the most productive activity, he felt, that he had engaged in the past month.

But finally the physical pain outweighed the pain inside. Wincing and rubbing his forehead, Max sighed. This wasn't getting him anywhere.

A letter! he suddenly realized. *I'll write Elizabeth a letter, and I'll—I'll explain everything.*

Suddenly Max felt rejuvenated. A letter could do what he couldn't do himself. It could tell Elizabeth how much he loved her—and how, by staying away, he was showing that love the best way he knew how.

Galvanized by his task, Max sat down at his desk and ripped off a sheet of the creamy, businesslike stationery—with equally official letterhead—his father had provided boxes of it for him since he was old enough to write.

Dear Elizabeth, he began, his pen scratching against the thick, parchmentlike paper.

Suddenly he looked down. "Oh, what am I doing!" he wailed. The paper stared up at him like a twisted mirror. He couldn't send her something on *this*. This was the kind of paper you used for the stupid thank-you notes he was soon going to have to write in the hundreds with his lovely new wife, Lavinia.

"Creep!" Max hissed at himself, crumpling the paper into a ball and hurling it across the room.

He searched feverishly through his drawers for something simpler and more personal, finally locating some plain, unmarked paper. He heaved a sigh of relief.

My dearest Elizabeth, he began again, unable to keep his brimming feelings from spilling out even into the customary greeting.

I'm writing because it's the only thing I can think to do at this point. I have a few things to say, and I hope you will read this letter long enough to hear them, although Lord knows I don't deserve it. I have been a selfish jerk, and if you never wanted to see me or speak to me again, I would understand.

Max hesitated for a moment, chewing his pen. A little extreme, maybe, but it was exactly how he felt. And he owed it to Elizabeth to give her at least that much—the right to never see him again. *Which she might just go ahead and take anyway,* he thought miserably.

This morning on the steps, I acted abominably. You know I love you, and you know I would like nothing better than to hold and kiss you all of the time. But since I can't, I feel the honorable thing is to—the honorable thing is to—

The stuttering on the page simply repeated the stuttering in his head. *The honorable thing is to do what, you twit? To never talk to the girl you love again?*

18

But an equally compelling argument continued in his head. *If I talk to her, I'll destroy my family!* he thought desperately, thinking of his laughing sister and his studious, kind father. *I can't let that happen!*

Max looked down at what he had already written on the paper. Suddenly the black scratches seemed menacing—hieroglyphics that hid a terrible recipe for disaster.

Why are you writing this letter anyway, Max? the voice inside his head asked with a nasty edge. *Just so Elizabeth knows what a lovely, honorable bloke she's losing?*

Max groaned and crumpled the letter, putting his head on the desk with a bang. *Nice work, mate,* the voice sneered. *You try to convince yourself that you're doing this for Elizabeth's benefit, but you're really doing it for your own. So Elizabeth never thinks of you as a dodgy, despicable jerk for what you've done to her.*

Which she has every right to do, the voice continued.

Max looked up at the ceiling, helpless before the truth. Two tears slipped down his face.

You've got to let her hate you, Max, he told himself. *You've got to let her hate you so she can move on.*

Max looked around at his expensive sitting room—all the polished, overstuffed furniture unable to protect him from the bracing tide of the

19

truth. *You've got to be cold. Positively distant. No more being selfish. You're ice.*

Suddenly a thought popped into Max's mind. He let out a bitter, surprised laugh.

"I've been pretending to love a woman I don't for months," Max said aloud. "How hard can it be to pretend I *don't* love the woman I do?"

Vanessa tripped down the main staircase lightly, humming some tuneless line in her head that seemed to express all the evil delight she took in breaking the simplest rules in the Pennington House code, now that she knew for sure that she could never be fired.

She knew she was getting a little out of control, though. When her roommate Alice had burst white-faced into the room and informed Vanessa that Mary wanted to see her straightaway, Vanessa had merely popped off something breezy, like, "Wouldn't want the Queen Mary to explode with impatience, now, would we, girls?" It wouldn't do. The last thing she needed was Elizabeth or Alice suspecting that something was going on between her and the family—some reason that justified all her abominable slacking off these last few weeks.

Although Elizabeth has other things on her mind right now, Vanessa decided.

Just the thought of Elizabeth's ashen face was

enough to send Vanessa into another fit of anger. Running her hand down the cool wood of the banister, she pictured herself ripping off a section and using it as a club to beat Max with.

Or the earl.

How dare they treat us like they do? Vanessa thought furiously. *Like—like toys they can just stick in the cupboard when they're done.*

She reached the foyer, looking at the smooth marble floor she'd waxed just hours ago. *And it's mine too,* she thought, running her toe over the smooth surface. *That's the irony—all of this is* mine.

And I'm going to make the earl pay dearly for taking it away from me, she added silently.

Unbidden, Vanessa's first and last confrontation with the earl came back to her. It hadn't been a complete success—but it hadn't been an entire failure either.

When Vanessa had knocked on his office door, holding up the old black-and-white photograph of her mother with him, the earl had been totally devastated. White-faced, he had simply repeated that he could not answer her at this time.

"That's all right," Vanessa had sneered back. "I've got plenty of time."

The earl had been completely silent. Finally he had simply nudged the photograph away, back toward her, like it was something he simply had no use for, and sat down at his desk.

"You can try to pretend it's not true," Vanessa had said. "But it doesn't matter. You're my *father*. You used my mother and left her pregnant and alone . . . with me. I only found out about the affair when my mum died, lonely and miserable and dirt-poor at the beginning of this year. You're my father. You are. I've got proof! Photographs and love letters don't lie . . . unlike certain upstanding earls."

He had looked up angrily, giving her the full benefit of his steely gaze—a gaze Vanessa was sure was put to good use in parliamentary sessions. Despite her bravado a moment before, she had felt a distinct little shiver.

"It's not true, I tell you," the earl said. "I am *not* your father, Vanessa. But you must give me a little time to—resolve certain matters before you share what you think you know with anyone."

Vanessa had taken a seat across from him. "Don't think of doing anything funny, you creepy old man." It had given her such a thrill to finally call the earl the terrible names that had been running through her mind all these months! "I've got copies of everything about your affair with my mother filed with the bank," she lied. "If anything happens to me, they'll be mailed to the *Star* and the *Guardian*."

The earl gave a little bark of surprise. "Why, I'm sure you do," he said simply.

Vanessa had felt like leaping across the desk. How *dare* he look at her that way! Like she was some disgusting money-grubber!

"Keep your nasty thoughts to yourself," she'd spat. "It's *you* who's done something disgusting. Not I."

The earl simply looked at her.

"It's not your money I want," she continued evenly. "I want you to pay for what you did to my mother."

The earl had been looking toward the window, but he turned around quizzically. "Just what did I do to your mother—besides have this alleged affair?" he asked in surprise.

It was more than Vanessa could take. "Like you don't know!" she screamed. "Leaving her to—to rot her life away in some stink hole in the East End while you went about your own *affairs!*" The last word curdled sarcastically in her mouth.

The earl, Vanessa was proud to see, looked slightly shaken. "Vanessa, you must wait," he finally managed. "I am truly sorry for whatever happened to your mother, and we will talk. We will talk about everything. But you must give me a little time."

Vanessa snatched up the photograph and placed it back in the envelope where she'd been keeping it. "Don't think you can wheedle your way out of this," she said, wondering if she was losing too much ground in not insisting on going to the press right away. But if she did that, she'd—what? Vanessa didn't know what kept her from fulfilling her threat immediately, but she knew that for whatever reason, she couldn't until she'd gotten the answers she wanted from the earl. "I've waited my whole life, and I can wait some more."

"Good," the earl had said, his voice sounding like it was emerging from a long, dark tunnel.

Vanessa had turned at the door. "But I'm going to make you pay for *every last minute*," she had spat. "I can't wait for your *legitimate* children to know they have a half sibling! To know their father cheated on their mother. To know what you did to my mum!" With that, she had slammed the door behind her and headed down the hall.

"Vanessa!"

Vanessa jerked out of her reverie and looked at the door to the foyer. Her boss, Mary, stood there, and she looked like she was out for blood.

When Mary was angry, her voice deepened. "May I trouble you for a moment of your precious time, Vanessa?" Mary continued in her menacing boom.

"Max? Max!" Vanessa heard the earl calling from somewhere else in the house.

Suddenly tears sprang to Vanessa's eyes, and

she forgot all about defusing the bomb in front of her. *He's my bloody father too!* she thought. *Why won't he acknowledge me?*

That's why it's partly Elizabeth's own fault for getting involved with one of these rich boys, Vanessa thought. *And it's why I'm saying* sayonara *to James Leer, Max's best friend and a fellow richie, at the first opportunity.*

"We need to talk about your performance," Mary's voice cut in. She gestured for Vanessa to follow her and turned on her heel, leaving Vanessa in the empty foyer, her heart pounding and her ears ringing with shame and pain.

Vanessa looked down at the sparkling floor. *Maybe it's because I'm such a bad maid,* she thought, choking back a sudden flood of laughter—and tears.

Chapter Two

Tasting what felt like ashy, dry cinders in his mouth, Max finally forced himself to shower, change, and get ready to leave Pennington House for lunch with Lavinia and her friends. Looking at the blank, white expanse of his freshly shaven face, Max put his hand to the mirror, watching the steam fill in his reflection.

He couldn't help but wish he were *really* disappearing.

Hastily exiting the house—no Elizabeth, Vanessa, or earl in evidence, thankfully—Max got into his car and immediately switched off the radio. The last thing he needed was music pumping into his ears. The thoughts in his head were too loud already.

After pulling his car smoothly out onto the road that led straight to Lavinia's place, Max tried to make his mind as blank as possible. Before he knew it, he was approaching the long drive to Lavinia's door. Well, he hadn't disappeared—he hadn't even managed to run off. Max checked his watch. Damn. He was fifteen minutes early. That meant fifteen more minutes he'd have to spend in Lavinia's acidic presence before they were, mercifully, in public, where it was all a performance anyway.

Although technically, a week from now I'll have committed myself to spending the rest of my life in her presence, Max thought. He looked down at his hands—they looked grayish green, like the hands of a corpse. Max was neatly groomed and shaven, but he felt like he was slowly being embalmed.

Keep calm, mate, Max told himself as he pulled into the drive that led to Lavinia's uncle and aunt's sprawling manor house. *Keep her talking. Perhaps you can finally convince her to give this ridiculous scheme up once and for all.*

But despite his personal pep talk, Max wasn't optimistic.

Jingling his keys in his pockets, Max walked up to the stiff double doors. The dour, pudding-faced butler let him in, then informed him that "Miss Lavinia is still in her dressing room, sir." *If only we could keep her there permanently.* Max groaned inwardly.

After knocking twice on the fortresslike door that led to Lavinia's suite of rooms, Max turned the knob and let himself in. "Lavinia?" he called, hoping that she had mistakenly flushed herself down her gleaming porcelain toilet.

As he walked down the carpeted hallway, he could hear her voice faintly. "But the linen wrinkles so abominably," she was whining. "And I don't know that it really complements my winter complexion."

God, more wedding crap, Max thought. It seemed that Lavinia was capable of holding three-hour conversations about even the smallest details of the wedding, like gold or silver plating for the dessert forks or whether rubber or foam padding would be preferable for holding down the rich, sumptuous red rug that would lead up the aisle. *The aisle that's going to be my gangplank if I can't figure something out bloody quick,* Max thought grimly.

"Oh, Max!" Lavinia crowed, finally catching sight of him. The sun silhouetted her against the window so that Max couldn't read the expression on her face, though he could see that she was dressed only in a slip and heels and held a cell phone clamped firmly against her ear. Not even dressed—that meant even more waiting. Damn. "I'll be just a moment," Lavinia chirped, and Max nodded and took a seat in one of the small blue chairs by the double-paned windows. He loosened his tie, feeling faintly nauseated by the peach-and-cream theme that Lavinia had chosen for her rooms a few months ago. It was like suffocating inside a giant scone!

"Uh-huh," Lavinia responded to the disembodied voice somewhere at the other end of cellular space. "Uh-*huh*." She reached over for a small metal nail file on her bedside table and began to work on her free hand.

Charming girl I've chosen here, Max thought. *A real fascinating conversationalist.*

"Well, fix it, then!" Lavinia suddenly exploded, her face contorting in an ugly fury that made her look like one of the gargoyles hanging off an old cathedral. "Do your job, why don't you?"

And a lovely phone manner too, Max added to himself.

Without another word Lavinia snapped the phone shut and threw it across the room. It bounced off the mattress and appeared unharmed. Lavinia pouted. With her arms folded across her chest, she looked exactly like a four-year-old about to throw an obscene tantrum. *Or refuse to finish her vegetables before she gets her pudding,* Max thought.

"Well, looks like you're not the only useless person around here," Lavinia finally declared.

Max sighed, running his hands through his hair. Since he'd confessed to Lavinia that he was (1) in love with Elizabeth, not her, and (2) dearly wanted to call off the wedding, Lavinia had adopted an arch,

30

menacing, slightly frantic tone in all of her dealings with him, as if she were only barely restraining herself from raking his face over and over with her fingernails. *Well, I'd have more sympathy with her supposed humiliation if she weren't blackmailing me into going through with this awful sham of a wedding,* Max thought, looking at his wife to be.

"Oh, quit gaping, Max," Lavinia snapped, plucking up a half-empty pack of cigarettes—also a new habit—and lighting a cigarette with a flourish, blowing the first puff of smoke defiantly in his direction. "If you leave your mouth open that way, flies will go in."

Feeling her words press against his temples like a lead headdress, Max found himself unable to speak. After this scene how could they go out to lunch with her college friends who'd flown in for the wedding and pretend to be some lovey-dovey couple? And how could they go through the rest of their lives together? Was this what it was always going to be like—Lavinia baiting and snapping at him in revenge for not being the cardboard cutout she'd signed up for, in a series of opulently furnished rooms, until he died?

Perhaps some straight talk could help. "Lavinia," Max said, with some effort, "if you think I'm useless, why are you so eager to marry me? Why don't you use your mouth to explain that to me?" Max leaned

31

back with a satisfied grin. He'd worried about hurting her feelings during the beginning of his relationship with Elizabeth, but he was slowly learning that Lavinia didn't allow herself to be hurt—she always made sure that she hurt others first.

Lavinia had sat down across from him, looking off into space with annoyance, clearly not listening to him in the least. Now she turned to Max with the same face she had previously made for the unseen caller.

"If you think I'm going to let my fiancé run off with some stupid American maid," Lavinia said with no small amount of heat, "then you've got another thing coming!" She ground out the cigarette for emphasis in an ashtray that was already filled with half-crumpled butts.

Max again felt the hopelessness of his cause. One couldn't talk to Lavinia like she was a reasonable adult and wanted the things an adult wanted from marriage. Max had to recognize that she was a spoiled child, and she reacted the way any spoiled child would when another child picked up her discarded toy: she wanted the toy back, at any cost.

Just to keep it away from anyone else.

"But Lavinia," Max continued, trying to remain calm, "I don't love you. You don't even love me. All we've got to give each other is a world of unhappiness."

Max thought that was an especially effective phrase, *a world of unhappiness,* but Lavinia had already turned her attention back toward her voluminous closets. "What?" she asked distractedly, holding up a navy dress and a black dress against her body and checking her reflection critically in the full-length mirror. "Oh, Max, do stop being so tedious and hand me that comb, will you?"

Max looked to his left at the tortoiseshell comb and then back at Lavinia. He didn't make a move. It was time to bring out the big guns. "Lavinia, I don't want to marry you," he said flatly, with as much gravitas as he could muster.

This brought Lavinia's maneuvers to a halt. She turned to Max, threw both dresses on the bed, and came to stand in front of him so his eyes were about even with her flat, hard belly. He could even smell the harsh, too-sweet perfume that clung to all of her clothing.

"Max," Lavinia said icily. "The invitations have been sent. The gifts have been received. Princess *Stephanie* has promised to come. And you will be *standing* with me at the altar on Sunday whether you like it or not."

Max felt frozen in place, like a toy soldier.

Lavinia's words were even and clipped, like the earl's when he was speaking about matters of state. "Understand?" she finished.

Max was interrupted by the cell phone's ringing again. "Oh, damn," Lavinia said, striding across the room and flipping it into place with one swift gesture. "Hello?" she asked imperiously.

Max put his head in his hands. He could blackmail her *back*, he suddenly realized. But with what? Lavinia hadn't engineered any drug deals that he was aware of.

"That was the caterer," Lavinia said, flipping the phone closed and looking at him with a curiously blank expression. "There's been another scare in the beef market in Hartfordshire. We're junking the livers and switching to gravlax with capers for the second course."

Max felt wooden. Hadn't Lavinia heard a word he'd just said?

"Fine," he finally answered tonelessly.

Something else occurred to Max: he could run away. Why couldn't he just leave it all? Leave Elizabeth, leave Lavinia, leave the whole bloody mess behind. It would be the coward's way out, but that was still a *way*, wasn't it?

Max's conscience answered him immediately. *Well, first of all, you love Elizabeth. Leaving her in the dust would be even* more *hurtful to her than sticking with an engagement you had before you even met her, and it would permanently establish you as the rat you are—that is, if you haven't managed to sufficiently turn her off already. Second, Lavinia would still go through with her threat to destroy your family—the only difference is, you wouldn't be here to do anything to stop it.*

"I know you're thinking of how you can weasel out of this," Lavinia continued, buttoning her cuffs and straightening the collar on the silk blouse she'd finally chosen from the heap on her bed. "But your stupid nervous breakdowns are not my affair. My business is getting you to the church on time, in your tails, with a ring in your pocket. Understand?" she repeated.

What did she think he was, an idiot child? Max couldn't bring himself to answer. It was hopeless, he saw. Lavinia had decided to treat the situation as jitters on his part—even if the fact that she was blackmailing him somewhat belied the notion that he was only a little "nervous" about the upcoming nuptials.

"And if you don't," Lavinia continued in a radiator's even hiss, "I will reveal the fact that your father had an affair with the maid almost twenty years ago and has an illegitimate child, and your sister will not be allowed into society and your father will lose his place in Parliament."

Lavinia smiled a terrifying smile. This time she dispensed with her familiar "understand?"

"You're making a mistake," Max finally muttered,

feeling absolutely beaten. It was lost, he saw; all hope for him and Elizabeth was lost—and perhaps even hope for just him. "You're making a terrible, stupid mistake." He hoped. He had no idea whether or not Lavinia's bombshell was true. Had his father had an affair? It seemed unthinkable. But if it was true, the smirch on his father's character and his sister's reputation in London society would be too damaging. He couldn't risk calling her bluff. And there was no way he could ask his father about it. Even if it wasn't true, the rumor would destroy his family.

Lavinia had Max, plain and simple.

By now Lavinia was completely dressed—all that was left was for her to finish affixing her favorite pearl studs in her ears. She flipped her hair over one shoulder, gave herself one last reassuring glance in the mirror, and turned to Max with an unmistakable gleam of triumph in her ice blue eyes.

"Oh, I'm not making a mistake, Max," Lavinia said with evident satisfaction. "I'm preventing *you* from making one."

"Bones McCall is gay, Sarah," Victoria said, cinching the belt of one of sixteen-year-old Sarah Pennington's more grown-up party dresses so tightly that Sarah was afraid Victoria was going to completely split the delicate seams around her rib cage.

"Here, give me that," Sarah said with frustration, pulling her best friend toward her as if she were a model's assistant and adjusting the belt to a more reasonable fit. She gave her a little pat and pushed her back in the other direction. "Now go look."

As Victoria tottered across the room on slightly too small high heels to have a go at the full-length mirror, Sarah sighed and flopped back down on her bed.

"You really think he might be gay?" she asked. Since the minute Victoria had offered that as an explanation for Bones's highly unresponsive behavior, Sarah hadn't been able to think about anything else. While Victoria went through practically every item of clothing in her wardrobe, they had been arguing about it, Victoria on the side that it would explain everything and Sarah on the side that it wouldn't explain the electric thrill she felt every time she saw Bones, which she was convinced was not all one-sided.

"It's not that I *think* he's gay," Victoria said, giving up on the blue dress and reaching for some of Sarah's new denim dark-rinse jeans. "It's just that I'm saying that would explain everything."

Even though they had already gone through this conversation twice, Sarah needed to hear it again to believe it. "Explain *what?*" Sarah wailed.

Victoria sighed, turning around, with the jeans midhike around her hips. Sucking in her breath, she closed the button and exhaled uncomfortably. "Arggggh!" she cried.

"For God's sake, Vic, stop mummifying yourself and tell me why you think that Bones is gay!" Sarah nearly screamed.

Victoria kicked off the jeans as quickly as she could and pulled her own pants—which were considerably looser—back on. "Listen," Victoria said, while Sarah tried not to hyperventilate. "It would totally make sense. I mean, look at Bones. He's sixteen. A famous rock star. Totally hot. But he's not dating Charlotte Church. So what does he do? He keeps girls around from our school that everyone will think of as his girlfriend—"

"Like me?" Sarah interjected.

"Like you," Victoria continued, unruffled, "and then when he's old enough, he tells everyone that he's gay."

Sarah was getting very freaked out by Victoria's theories, especially since they echoed Sarah's own since she'd met Bones McCall. The teen rock star had transferred to the Welles School, and Sarah had immediately made a play for him. They'd become fast friends, but Bones had never tried anything. Nothing. Nada.

Sarah sighed, her gaze taking in her destroyed

bedroom. Victoria had thrown practically every item in her wardrobe around the room. It looked like a small bomb had gone off. If Max saw it, he would have a cow. *Actually, what would Max care?* Sarah suddenly thought, realizing how soon the wedding was. *In another week this won't even be his house anymore.* The thought made her feel lonely and very, very cold—the only inhabitant of an airless gray planet. Her brother was her only savior in this boring house.

"Vic, get me my black skirt," Sarah snapped, standing up. She suddenly knew what she had to do. She had a plan.

Victoria looked at Sarah like she was slowly growing another head. "Sarah . . . what are you thinking?" she asked uneasily.

"Oh, just do it!" Sarah snapped. She didn't want to be distracted from her scheme for one minute—if she thought about it for too long, she might lose her nerve. Sarah didn't even notice when Victoria wordlessly handed over the straight black pencil skirt the two had found together at Semblance, a hot new Soho store, over the fall vacation.

Bones likes me, Sarah was thinking. *And better yet, he's not a total jerk like some other people I could name. So tonight I'm just going to take the pressure off him and make the first move. He has girls throwing themselves at him all the time—it makes sense that he'd be cautious. But he likes me. I know it.*

"Sarah! Sarah! Earth to Sarah!" Victoria was saying, waving her hands in front of Sarah in an unsuccessful bid for her attention.

And tonight I'm going to make sure that he knows I like him too, Sarah thought.

Elizabeth wanted to strangle herself with her feather duster.

For the past two hours she had been assigned the bric-a-brac in the drawing room. *And the bric-a-brac in this drawing room would fill a small ocean liner,* she thought miserably, attempting to squat down so that her neck wouldn't be sacrificed to her task along with her arms and eyes, which were already grimy and choked with dust.

"A term paper. A term paper. My kingdom for a term paper," Elizabeth muttered to herself hoarsely, regretting the days that she'd ever considered plotting a twenty-page treatise on *King Lear* onerous in the least.

It wasn't only the delicate china and countless glass baubles that were giving Elizabeth serious stomach pains. For the past half hour she'd been forced to listen to wedding planner Niles Neesly in an adjacent room holding what seemed like an endless series of meetings with the various parties hired to make the wedding between Lavinia and

Max a day to make Queen Victoria wish she could rise from the grave and attend.

"So we're all agreed?" Niles trilled at some unfortunate group of individuals.

Are we agreed that it's faintly catastrophic that I slept with the groom? Elizabeth asked herself, giving a set of Chinese vases a particularly vigorous going-over.

The heinosity had been going on for hours. First, Niles had given the string quartet that was to gently accompany the prewedding cocktail party a grilling worthy of a disciple of Leonard Bernstein. "The Bach must not be stuffy!" he had shrilled, forcing Elizabeth to picture him with a small baton atop a podium. "The Bach must encourage the guests to look forward to the ceremony approaching, while preparing them for both the joy and the gravitas of the situation."

God, what a gasbag, Elizabeth had thought, wishing she could shatter one of the small Dresden shepherdesses, knowing that the musicians would surely appreciate any distraction from the balding, screaming man in front of them. Thank God she wasn't on Vanessa's detail—which was to bring Niles and his minions any refreshment they might desire.

But it had gotten worse. After dismissing the string quartet—who hurried through the drawing room as if the very hounds of hell were at their heels—Niles had welcomed in the wedding's ushers, who had already been forced to physically go through the wedding's twenty- to eighty-million phases with Niles at least thirty-seven thousand times.

"You are here to *what?*" Niles had brayed.

"To expedite," the tribe repeated dully, having already learned that where Niles Neesly was concerned, agreement was the better part of valor.

"And to *what?*" Niles had pressed on.

To exterminate! Elizabeth wanted to scream from the next room, knowing that if she did so, the beleaguered ushers would join her in ripping Niles Neesly neatly into shreds.

It was ridiculous, Elizabeth thought. She had left California to make a better, new life for herself, free from all these bizarre love triangles, and all she had done was find herself at the center of the mother of all love triangles since the beginning of time. *And I can safely say,* Elizabeth thought, *that having your sister seduce your boyfriend is completely preferable to waiting on the bride at the wedding of your lover.*

Argh! Elizabeth thought, finally reaching the end of an impossibly long row of fragile glass flowers, which she restrained herself from popping into her mouth and chewing whole into little shards.

Well, when these flowers are Lavinia's, she can find someone else to dust them, Elizabeth thought. *I'll be long gone.*

Suddenly Elizabeth had a disquieting thought. For the past month or so she had been doing a good job of completely *not* thinking of Jessica and Sam and their betrayal. Of course, losing her virginity to Max and then tiptoeing around him like he was one of the china shepherdesses—*Without any different vibe on his side, thanks very much,* Elizabeth thought sourly—had been a significant distraction, but still. Why had she never realized that she was doing exactly what she had found so hateful in Jessica?

In the next room there was a shift as papers were shuffled and some new group entered for Niles's instructions. Elizabeth felt a sickly kick in her stomach. *Is this how Jessica felt?* Elizabeth thought, holding the feather duster in her hand like a wounded bird.

The thought had such a terrible power that Elizabeth was forced to sit down for a moment in one of the silk-upholstered chairs that she had labored over the day before. She stroked the dark wood of the arms with her fingertips, feeling that the intensity of her thoughts might radiate to the tips of her fingers, boring smooth gouges in the filigreed wood.

And did Jess love Sam so much that she just wanted to x me out of the universe? Elizabeth wondered, hearing the clatter of new bottoms settling into folding chairs like the roaring of a distant train. *The way I want to do to Lavinia?*

Elizabeth let the duster drop from her dirty knees to the floor, looking blankly at the shining row of cherubs she had finished hours before.

It would make sense, Elizabeth thought, her reporter's instinct keeping her from blocking out any unpleasant thought that seeped, like so much water, into her consciousness. *If she really loved Sam, that is.* But Elizabeth doubted that Jessica did love—or had loved—Sam Burgess. It simply made no sense.

Abruptly Vanessa poked her head into the doorway, jolting Elizabeth out of her reverie. "Working hard, I see," Vanessa joked.

Elizabeth tried to smile. "Just contemplating a vacation from this house. A *permanent* one."

Vanessa looked surprised, then pleased. She gave Elizabeth a shy, almost feline smile—one of the rare ones Elizabeth had ever seen Vanessa dispense. "You and me both, Elizabeth."

As Sarah mounted the steps to Bones's parents' palatial digs in London, she waved off her driver, Fenwick, with a sigh of exasperation. Ever since her brief dalliance with the disastrous Nick this past summer, her father had declared that Sarah was not allowed to leave the house except to see *certain friends*—which Sarah knew meant, in the earl's tortured syntax, people of the same class and breeding as herself. Luckily Bones's titled parents made him fit neatly into the category, and despite his pop-star status, the earl was pleased to have Sarah develop a relationship with the young scion.

The McCalls' butler led Sarah through the labyrinth of the huge house to the "media room," where Bones was waiting for her with a ready grin on his gorgeous face.

"Everything's set up, *chica*," he whispered, pointing upward to where his parents, presumably, were sleeping in their second-floor bedroom. "Have a seat and in mere moments we'll be watching one of our favorite movies."

The huge cave of an entertainment room was lined with six-foot-tall speakers, plush leather couches, and a wide-screen TV. The coffee table was groaning with every manner of junk food: crisps, Cadbury bars, Hit biscuits.

As Bones fiddled with a huge master control that looked like it could power the entire tube, Sarah snuck little side glances at him. She could barely contain herself. *Now I just have to implement step two of the master plan*. As surreptitiously as she could, she reached into her pocket for the foreign object that was going to secure things between the two of them for sure. It was still there. Sarah breathed a sigh of relief, like she had touched a magic talisman.

"Lights dimmed or off?" Bones asked, with what Sarah took to be a mischievous grin, dangling the remote from his hands.

"Oh, off," she responded playfully.

He plopped down next to her, his thigh almost touching hers, and they dug into the food and leaned back to watch *Scary Movie*. Sarah munched her way through two packets of Hits, knowing she was going to regret it the minute she went home, but she was totally too nervous to let her hands just rest at her sides. Through the entire procedure, though, Sarah was acutely aware of Bones's every breath, of his proximity to her, how if he just turned *ever so slightly* to his left, their lips would meet perfectly in midair.

As the last tape rewound to an end and Sarah started to gather up her things, she fumbled in her pocket for the key to her master plan. It was a sprig of mistletoe, filched from the wedding arrangements, which, as the Christmas season demanded, were literally bursting with the plant. *As if we need any more goony kissing around our house*, Sarah thought, thinking with dread of the upcoming nuptials.

"Ten already!" Bones said, eyeing the clock on the wall. "Fenwick will be waiting outside," he added as he stood, that adorable smile on his face. "I had such a fun time with you as usual, Sar."

Sarah whipped the mistletoe out of her back pocket like a concealed weapon. Smiling meaningfully in Bones's general direction, she dangled the plant over both their heads. "Look what my stupid brother's stocked the house with for his wedding," Sarah said, and closed her eyes in preparation for the deep, soulful touching of tongues that was surely to follow.

But—after a frightening, chilling silence—all she felt was a cool, dry kiss on her cheek, leaving a faint whiff of Bones's pleasant, soapy smell in its wake. She opened her eyes. Bones was smiling at her but was also clearly done.

Dammit! Sarah thought, wanting to scatter all the uneaten junk food around the room in a fit of rage. *What do I have to do to get a decent snog around here?*

However, there was no way she was going to show Bones her frustration. She tried to force a cackle to her throat to hide her disappointment. "Got to practice for all those old cadavers pinching my cheeks at the wedding, you know," she joked.

Bones was walking with her to the door. *He was walking her to the bleeding door!* He snuck a glance behind Sarah, as if she was being followed by elves.

"Yes—protect *all* your cheeks," he said, grinning widely. "Especially from the archdukes. My mother always says they're the worst."

Sarah wanted to wail with frustration. As Bones opened the massive door, letting in a cool blast of air, to reveal a waiting Fenwick, Sarah was glumly forced to concede that her big plan had been a bust.

"Vell, a pleasure, as alvays," Bones said, reaching for Sarah's hand and touching it lightly to his lips. He opened his mouth and gave his imitation of a Dracula-like laugh, deep, booming, and spooky. At this moment Sarah would have settled for a Dracula-like bloodletting—anything! But there was nothing forthcoming except the old prep-school runaround. "I look forward to your next call, milady," Bones said, letting go of her hand.

"And I to yours," Sarah responded prettily, even working up the gumption for a little curtsy, though she was far from in the mood to flirt and act nice. In fact, in her present state it was all she could manage. Turning abruptly, she ran down the stairs to Fenwick and slammed the car door behind her as hard as she could.

All the way home to Pennington House, Fenwick was thankfully silent, leaving Sarah to her own thoughts. She had very few, except that maybe Victoria was right—Bones *was* gay. *Or just doesn't fancy me,* Sarah thought, trying to stifle the cavernous depths of despair that that particular thought seemed to open up right in the middle of her chest, like her emotions were performing an autopsy on her.

Back at Pennington House, Sarah ran away from the car and up to her room as quickly as she could, silently thankful that the earl wasn't lurking around for a late night update and that she could wait until tomorrow to tell Victoria of her failure—when surely it would hurt less. She got ready for bed silently, flossing her teeth with deliberation and sliding between her crisp sheets. She could still feel the shape of Bones's lips on her hand, a little electric burn that wouldn't stop tingling, even though she'd washed her hands three times under hot water.

Chapter Three

Max thought he was being woken by Lavinia in her wedding dress.

He had been having the dream he'd had almost every night for the past four weeks. In it Lavinia appeared in the distance, a tiny white dot, like the Good Witch approaching in her pink bubble in *The Wizard of Oz*.

But every night, as she got closer, Max realized she was hurtling toward him at breakneck speed, not floating in some suspended shimmering bubble. "Nooo!" Max always cried in vain, his arms held straight out in front of him to ward her off before he was smashed like a water balloon and enveloped by an enormous, suffocating cloud of white.

Which was when he normally woke up.

"Good Lord, Max," Lavinia said, her palms

clamped against the hard wood of the bedroom door. "What's wrong with you?"

Max shook himself completely awake. Lavinia had been reaching toward him . . . no, floating . . . then suddenly her talons had been clutching his shoulders . . . shaking him until he thought he was going to die. . . .

"Sorry, Lav," Max gasped, sitting up straight in bed. "I was having a bad dream."

"I'll give you a bad dream," Lavinia snapped. Her eyes were as wide as two saucers. She was wearing all white, which Max was sure was the cause of him thinking she was the terrible, hurtling Lavinia in the dream, thus causing his only partially wakened self to reach out and shove her across the room. White silk pants and a white blouse, her hair pulled back with a spray of baby's breath, Max noted, looking over Lavinia more carefully. Was this supposed to be some subtle reminder of events to come? In any case, it had backfired. Max tried not to grin.

"Really sorry, Lav," Max said, throwing back the covers with one movement and glancing at the clock. It was only 7:05 A.M. What was Lavinia doing here?

"What's going on?" Max asked, hoping against hope that Lavinia had had an early morning change of heart and had come over to the house to spontaneously break the engagement. *In that outfit, it's not likely,* Max told himself with a sinking feeling. Lavinia was very chic, and she *always* dressed for the occasion—the breaking of a long-term engagement would certainly necessitate black, preferably crepe.

Lavinia recovered herself and strode confidently across the room, leaning down to finger the collar of Max's flannel pajamas. Max flinched—he couldn't help it. "Why, I came to have an early morning breakfast with you, my darling!" Lavinia said without sarcasm.

Max couldn't shake the thought that Lavinia—for all her tricks and chicanery—had no idea, really, what she was doing. How else could she be so creepily blind to how Max felt about her, in even the smallest ways? As in, he'd rather eat a live turtle than have breakfast with her. "You what?" he asked stupidly.

"Get in the shower, you ape," Lavinia said cheerfully. "I've come to breakfast with you and your family, but I'd like you presentable, at least."

Faced with such an onslaught of precocious decisiveness, half-awake Max had no choice but to obey. Perhaps, in fact, this was only a new version of the dream, and he was still sleeping. "Breakfast—with me?" he asked, just to be sure. Could this be some formal matrimonial ceremony that he wasn't really required to attend, like the wedding breakfasts in Edith Wharton novels?

"No, I came to break bread with the maid you want to shag," Lavinia said curtly. "Get in the shower, Max, before I toss you in in your pajamas."

Max became completely awake. This was Lavinia, all right, and he wasn't having a dream. Unfortunately.

"Be just a moment," he said, disappearing into the bathroom. Standing under the stream of hot water, he contemplated ways to get out of the situation, going so far as to consider the bathroom window as he shaved. It was a large, many-paned entrance that he could fit through easily. Unfortunately, it was flush with the absolutely straight front of the house, and it was a nearly forty-foot drop to the ground. *And I'd just have to get married on crutches,* Max thought, picturing himself in a crumpled heap among the scrubby bushes lining the drive.

When he emerged from a cloud of steam, Lavinia was still there, a brown leather purse angled across her shoulder and waist. She was paging through one of his history journals.

"God, Max, I don't know how you stand this rubbish," Lavinia said, flinging the book aside with a harrumph.

The same way I stand you, of course, Max choked

54

down. *The same way I stand doing everything I'm "supposed" to do.*

He dressed quickly while Lavinia made notes in her leather wedding journal—*Organizing valets by height, no doubt,* Max couldn't help thinking. As the two descended, Max could see that his father and an especially sulky Sarah were already assembled at the breakfast table. The earl peered over his crisply opened *Times.*

"Why, who is this angel descended into our midst?" asked the earl rhetorically.

Lavinia actually simpered in response—it made Max sick to watch it. He was relieved to see Sarah looking a bit green too.

"Oh, *Father,*" Lavinia said simply. Sarah looked like she wanted to take one of the teacups off its saucer and bash Lavinia's head in with it.

"Now, what brings your divine presence into our midst this morning?" the earl asked.

Max sighed and held out a chair for Lavinia, easing himself into the one next to her. Could that terrible story Lavinia was carrying around about the earl have any truth to it at all? Was it possible that his father *had* seduced someone and had a child out of wedlock?

Max glanced at his father, who at that moment was holding his butter knife happily above his china plate, waiting with rapt, hypercivilized attention for Lavinia's answer. It was impossible to envision the earl of Pennington buying a liter of milk, much less seducing someone, Max thought. So what was he so afraid of?

"Oh, I just thought I'd come and see the man I love," Lavinia answered prettily. Max noticed that she didn't look at *him* when she said it. *Perhaps all our problems would be solved if Father ran off with Lavinia, at that,* Max thought, losing whatever dregs of appetite he had retained for breakfast at that moment.

"Tell me what's happening at work," the earl said to Lavinia, and she began to chatter on about her job at the auction house while Sarah heaved an audible sigh. Max reached for a slice of dry, chewy toast. He wanted to wink across the table at Sarah, but he couldn't catch her eye. He joined her in another sigh. Just another ordinary breakfast at Pennington House.

"Eggs?" Max heard, from somewhere in the neighborhood of his left shoulder.

Max closed the newspaper and looked up into the beautiful eyes of Elizabeth Bennet.

"Poached, p-please," he finally stammered.

Elizabeth made a note on her pad, then moved on to Sarah. "Eggs?" she repeated.

Max watched her leave him, then physically jerked himself back around to his paper. As usual, on seeing Elizabeth, he had only wanted to plant his lips on hers. He thought of their recent kiss under the mistletoe, and his breath came faster while he could feel a flush creeping onto his face. He was disturbed by something else too, although he tried not to show it. Usually looking into Elizabeth's eyes gave him an electric shock—a shock he could tell was felt by both of them. This time, however, it had been strangely one-sided. This time, staring into Elizabeth's eyes had been like staring into the glassy, thoughtless face of a clock.

Who, Max wondered, *replaced Elizabeth with a figurine from Madame Tussaud's?*

From his peripheral vision he could observe Elizabeth taking orders from Lavinia and the earl, her ponytail swinging from side to side as she walked. *Dammit—why does she have to be so beautiful?* Max thought helplessly.

Elizabeth closed her pad with an efficient bang and shoved it into her back pocket. She looked like she could be considering yogurt flavors in the grocery store—she looked, in fact, like a waitress at her job, a job she didn't care about except for her paycheck, particularly. Max felt a stab somewhere in the region of his stomach, and it traveled up his throat, making him regret his few sips of coffee and bites of doughy toast. *Has Elizabeth given me up, then?* he asked himself, too despairing to stop himself from looking at her through little peeks, just in case she came alive and began to transmit that she was the warm, vibrant Elizabeth he knew and loved.

Through the haze of Lavinia's endless chatter with the earl, Max's thoughts sounded like dull gongs tolling the end of day. *Of course she's given you up, mate,* Max answered himself. *Or have you forgotten the small detail of your impending wedding . . . and the fact that you've given Elizabeth no cause to hope?*

Elizabeth had almost stumbled as she entered the sunny dining room. She had prepared herself for the onslaught of Max: his winking, adorable eyes; his shock of dark hair; his crisp collar rising up above his lordly neck. What she hadn't expected to see was Lavinia, all in white like it was the wedding already.

Elizabeth! she scolded herself, willing herself into a mask that was as difficult to maintain as a stretch of the smooth desert earth of Death Valley on a hot, baking day. *Just keep it together, will you?* she grumbled, wishing she hadn't forced down a bowl of farina at breakfast. Now that she'd seen Lavinia, the thought of the white, pasty slop with its jellied edges was making her sick.

As Elizabeth had approached Lavinia for her

egg order, she'd forced herself not to look at her. But avoiding her eyes turned out not to be a problem—Lavinia was consumed with the earl anyway.

"My dear, we are all positively agog with anticipation," the earl was saying to her, leaning across the table to give her an affectionate pat on the hand.

Agog with anticipation? Elizabeth thought snarkily. *When has the earl ever put so many words together in a coherent sentence? I thought he just knew how to say, "That will be all," like he was some schizoid prophet or something.*

"Poached," Elizabeth heard, as if from some distant, echoing star system a million light-years away. "Poached, poached, poached, poached."

Suddenly Elizabeth heard a giggle. She came back to herself. She was staring straight into the blond, heartless face she feared the most: Lavinia's.

"Is there some problem?" Lavinia asked icily.

"Poached," Elizabeth heard herself repeating. "Absolutely."

"So I've got the reception outfit laid out already in my sitting room," Lavinia was saying from very far away. She turned back to the earl, Elizabeth's domestic error having been accounted for and dismissed. "Isn't that silly? But I can't wait until it's over and I've put it on. . . ." Lavinia's voice trailed off.

Elizabeth stood behind the earl. *Now, that's a*

sentiment I can get behind, she thought. *This entire thing being over and behind us all . . . forever.*

Vanessa was right! Elizabeth suddenly realized with a shock, thinking of how her coworker had urged her again and again to get away from Max, to really and truly separate herself from the Pennington family and everything it represented. *I need to get away from here,* she thought. *I need to get away from here and put this whole thing behind me.*

Elizabeth felt the epiphany with all the force of a slug shattering a wall of glass. Her thoughts were moving so fast, she was having a hard time keeping track of them. *You came from here to get away from everything,* Elizabeth told herself, feeling the misery seep through her bones like ink into cotton at how little that particular ideal had been reached. *But you just got yourself into another mess. And now you have to keep your chin up and find some way to make the next place not be a disaster area.*

As much as Elizabeth wanted to believe her optimistic thoughts, she knew she was being drawn in two directions—back home and to the garret of Pennington House. She really, really didn't want to go anywhere else. "None," she heard herself respond to the earl's clipped, "None for me, thanks."

Home, she told herself, her heart opening to the pain the man seated directly opposite was causing her. *I want to go home.*

It couldn't be worse than it is right here, could it? Elizabeth asked herself faintly.

"Elizabeth," she heard, her name taking on an edge in whoever's mouth had formed the four syllables. She swiveled in Sarah's direction. Sarah was holding up her teacup with a scornful expression. Elizabeth nodded, and in that moment she lost it.

Like a magnetic beam, Max's eyes were drawing hers to his.

Helpless, Elizabeth let all the feeling that she had been stifling pour across the table into Max's plaintive gaze, which seemed to carry enough voltage to power half of England. *I know it's awful,* Max's gaze seemed to be saying. *But what can I do?*

Nothing, Elizabeth's gaze responded, like a sign blinking No Vacancy. *Everything Nothing. Everything.*

The spell between them was broken by a scream from Lavinia, which, like a wave, crashed on everyone's ears, then receded into a thin ebb. "The help! I would like the help to be assembled . . . immediately." Lavinia trailed off as she realized that everyone was scared into silence at her screech.

Elizabeth felt nothing but a dull acceptance. So she was finally going to be fired: publicly, humiliatingly. And Max, of course, would—and could—do nothing to stop it.

That wasn't quite true. Max turned to Lavinia.

61

"Lavinia . . . what are you doing?" he asked—taking care, Elizabeth noted with no little asperity, to keep his voice bland, nonthreatening, as if he were dealing with an uncaged Bengali tiger.

"You'll see," Lavinia said crisply, taking the little bell that the Penningtons rarely used—Sarah preferred to shout—from the middle of the table and ringing it as if a hurricane were approaching. "Mary! Alice! Vanessa! I'm so glad you could join us," she said smoothly as the help clattered up from the kitchen and filed into the dining room, looking as apprehensive as Elizabeth felt.

"I have an announcement to make," Lavinia announced.

If Lavinia insists I be let go, Elizabeth thought, *I don't have to worry. I have almost seven hundred pounds saved up from this job already. I can afford a night in a bed-and-breakfast in London. Then I can scan the help-wanted ads, decide what I'm going to do next.*

"It concerns Elizabeth," Lavinia continued, her consonants crisp and sparkling.

"Lavinia," Max hissed in one last-ditch effort.

Well, no one can say you didn't give saving me your all, Max, Elizabeth thought bitterly. She forced herself to look straight into Lavinia's eyes. *This girl,* Elizabeth thought, trying to rationalize Max's weakness, *is a monster, and she's not going to be satisfied until she's eaten me alive. I never had a chance against her, and neither does Max. He has to hold the family honor together. When—if—I ever forgive Max, I'm going to try to remember that.*

"Miss," Mary broke in, causing all the servants to swivel suddenly in her direction, as if she had changed the chemical composition of the room. Elizabeth felt a little bell go off in her head. *Why, Mary's going to defend me!* Elizabeth thought, pleasure and surprise rising in her limbs like sap. *Or she's going to stop Lavinia from tearing me limb from limb before we've all eaten lunch, at least. Which is no small thing.*

"Perhaps this is best discussed," Mary went on, hesitating like a beachcomber clambering over slick rocks, "in the privacy of my office."

But Lavinia was positively ruthless, and she popped Mary's suggestion into her mouth like a cherry tomato. "Why, not at all," she said, exhibiting a smile that showed all of her teeth. "I think it's best I share this with everyone."

Mary was stunned into silence—*She has her job to think about, after all,* Elizabeth thought, still strangely touched. All of the breakfast inhabitants stood like prisoners, locked in Lavinia's next move.

"I would like Elizabeth," Lavinia slowly said, each word falling like a jagged bit of glass from her mouth, "to serve at my table at the wedding."

There was a brief moment of silence while all of the listeners digested this information. Elizabeth was the last to, finding herself wondering if "serve at my table at the wedding" might also mean "to be served on the table at the wedding—medium rare, preferably."

But suddenly Mary, Alice, and Vanessa were taking Elizabeth's hands in their own and shaking them vigorously, and Elizabeth knew from the relief in their gestures that somehow she had been saved. *But saved for what?* she asked herself. Something even worse, perhaps? Confirming her fears, Vanessa whispered, "You've dodged a bullet," in Elizabeth's ear before disappearing back through the swinging door with the rest of the help.

Elizabeth forced a smile. She'd have to talk to the ice queen, after all—talk before she was thrown to the wolves. "I'd be delighted," she said, wondering if she had time to escape before the earl could lay another "that will be all" on her.

Max, Elizabeth observed, had been reduced to a crumpled heap in the corner. Elizabeth tried to reestablish the contact they had felt in the moment before Lavinia had halted everything with her screech. But Max would have none of it. Slowly he raised the paper over his head, disappearing behind it like a mole burrowing into his hovel.

If that's the way you want it, Elizabeth thought, blinking back the tears stinging her eyes. *Don't let the bastards get you down,* she thought, comforted by Vanessa's words to her earlier, regarding the spinning wheel of chance that ruled the affections of the Pennington clan.

"Quite an honor, Elizabeth," the earl said, turning very slightly to face her, like a turtle that could only crane his head in one direction. "I'll be sure to remember it in your paycheck."

Elizabeth smiled quickly and escaped into the tiled hallway, breathing against the freshly painted walls for a moment before she entered the kitchen, preparing the stiff mask of formality that would replace her face again as soon as she came into sight of her coworkers.

After the sickening spectacle of Elizabeth's humiliation by Lavinia that all the servants had been forced to witness that morning, Vanessa was having a hard time keeping her fingers off the telephone to London's *Buzz,* the insolent gossip rag that traded in the secrets of the wealthy and powerful.

The fact that *Buzz* was a lever she could use to her advantage had only penetrated her brain during her confrontation with the earl. *I'm sure you do,* echoed in her brain. The fact that the earl assumed she was only out for the money still filled her with a white-tinged, glittering rage.

You'd never do anything just for the money, would you, Vanessa? she asked herself.

But Vanessa was too upset and worried about Elizabeth—and herself—to allow the self-destructive voice that lodged in her brain to gain much purchase. *Yeah—like I'd get any money from exposing the earl for his scandal,* Vanessa thought. *They'd give me fifty thousand pounds, and then I'd spend it all on my first lawyer—the one I'd need for the massive lawsuit the earl would immediately bring against me for libel.*

Vanessa breathed in and out deeply, trying to calm herself down. She held the cool plastic receiver to her face. *You're not doing this for money, Vanessa,* she told herself. *You're doing it because Max is clearly doing the same thing to Elizabeth that the earl did to your mother.*

"And they can't be allowed to get away with it," Vanessa muttered aloud.

It made her sick. *I mean, where did these gits get off?* Did they really think that the girls who worked—who were *forced* to work, Vanessa qualified—in their houses constituted nothing so much as their own private harem? Did they think the girls enjoyed their employers' abuse? Did they not really think about it much either way?

They don't think about it, Vanessa decided, *any more than they think about what kind of sandwich they'd like to have with their tea.*

No, her inner critic responded, remembering all the times she'd brought a tray the earl had rejected back to the kitchen to be "corrected." *Actually, they give a great deal of thought to whether they'd like wheat or rye.*

Revved up by her anger, Vanessa dialed the first three numbers of the *Buzz's* toll-free gossip line. Losing her nerve suddenly, she slammed the receiver back down.

C'mon, darling. Don't be scared. It's not like the earl's exactly been banging down your door with baby pictures and pledges to do right by you, has he?

Vanessa took a deep breath and dialed again. This time she waited until the line connected—fearing in her paranoia that the voice at the other end of the line would be the earl's, as if he had set up a special phone loop to divert calls of this nature.

I really should be calling from outside the house, Vanessa thought miserably, feeling an immediate sheen of sweat dampen the cheap cotton of her work shirt.

She was strangely startled by the live, human voice that greeted her at the other end of the line—it was as if one of the sculptures in the garden had started speaking. "Get the buzz," a rough voice—a voice that had clearly gone through quite a few pints and packs of cigarettes—answered. Vanessa immediately hung up the phone.

Stop being such a ninny! Vanessa screamed at herself. *Just tell the lady what you know and hang up the phone!*

As if she were performing delicate brain surgery, Vanessa dialed the series of numbers again. She listened to the short buzzes. The same lady picked up.

"Get the buzz," the rough voice answered.

Vanessa hung up again. She couldn't help it. The lady didn't care—she knew it. This was clearly some secretary that answered the phone the same way eighty-eight thousand times a day. She didn't care about the earl or Vanessa's mother. She was going to transfer the call to some editor. People hung up on her, and she took it as part of the territory. She was just doing her job.

Just like Vanessa.

Not like Vanessa, Vanessa whispered to herself.

Vanessa leaned back into the cool sheets—the sheets that she'd changed that morning, in fact. *You need to keep a cool head,* she told herself. *The earl is keeping a cool head, and he has friends in high places. He has friends that could—take care of—an unfortunate daughter.*

It suddenly struck Vanessa just how alone she

was—not only emotionally, but *legally,* of all the ridiculous things. *If the earl wants to take me out, I'm toast,* she thought, picturing a corpse-white Vanessa drifting to the bottom of the ocean, held down by cement blocks.

Don't be ridiculous, Vanessa scolded herself. *This isn't some Mafia movie, and the earl is a member of Parliament.*

That won't stop him from doing all he can to stop me, Vanessa's inner critic cautioned.

Suddenly Vanessa realized she did know a lawyer, after all. She let out a bitter laugh.

James, she thought. *I could ask James for advice.*

Vanessa turned over on the bed, looking out onto the rolling grounds of Pennington House. As she never had before, she felt the relative weakness of her position, her puny insignificance in the steamroller face of a prominent family like the Penningtons.

You can let them steamroll you like you're some little bug, Vanessa thought, thinking of James's seemingly honest, hopeful face. She thought of going to him, putting forth her case, and asking him—as she had never asked anyone before—for his help.

A surge of rage rose up in her so hot that Vanessa was forced to bury her head in the pillow.

Or you can stick yourself in another viper's nest, Vanessa thought.

Chapter Four

Sarah was pretending she was a private investigator.

It was the morning following her debacle with Bones, and she had dedicated herself—as much as it pained her—to finding out, once and for all, whether he was, in point of fact, really as gay as the day was long.

"Watch for a little too much bum patting," Victoria had urged that morning after Sarah had apprised her of her plans. "Also—any fashion moves that don't appear to come from his manager."

"Will you get your pathetic carcass away from me," Sarah had hissed in response.

So far, anyway, the morning had been a bust. There had been *no* Bones sightings—none to speak of. Had he repaired to his bedchamber, overwhelmed by his idiotic actions the night before?

Was he holed up in some flowery glen with Phillipa, Sarah's archenemy at school?

Or *Phillip*?

Sarah crashed out of her English seminar, her nerves ringing like the clanging of twelve o'clock. She didn't even want to consider how she had maintained that Hamlet's name had something to do with the charming nature of small country villages. She didn't want to remember how she'd declared aggressively that Gertrude, for all her weirdness, really had married Hamlet Senior's brother out of true love, not a desire to maintain her place in the Danish kingdom.

She didn't want to remember how she'd referred to Gertrude as "Lady Macbeth."

Sarah slunk passed the crowds of chattering students, wanting to hold her books up across her face like a shield. She tried to breathe naturally.

Just three more classes and I'm out of here, she thought, thinking of the cool black interior of the car, of Fenwick's stable, unquestioning presence, driving her swiftly back to her room, where she could bury her head in her hands and weep in peace.

Suddenly, however, all her plans changed.

Like an oasis rising up out of the dry, arid desert, she saw Bones.

Bones! she had to keep herself from crying

aloud down the packed hallway. *Wherefore have thou been, all these long and empty hours?*

Bones was leaning up against a locker, talking to Phillipa. Phillipa, Sarah observed nastily and with pleasure, was wearing a blue skirt that was much too tight.

No, it doesn't suit, Sarah thought, gliding toward the couple silently so she could observe—or not observe—as many signs of sexuality as she could muster.

"I liked Stankonia," she could hear Bones observing as she drew closer. "But I really think that Radiohead had the album of the year—no contest."

He's not talking about flower arrangements! Sarah thought with glee. *And he almost has his arm around Phillipa.*

Sarah observed the arm in question as closely as she dared. No—it definitely wasn't placed randomly up on the locker. It was descending toward Phillipa with determination, like a ball that had been thrown up in the air, stayed suspended for a moment, then yielded to the ineluctable force of gravity.

Sarah had to laugh at herself. *Who knew,* she thought, *that the day would come when I would be thrilled to see Bones flirting with Phillipa?*

But her elation was followed quickly—snapping at its heels like a rabid dog—by an unbelievable stab of pain. *Maybe Bones didn't leave me alone because he's gay,* Sarah thought, feeling like all her oxygen was being cut off by the descent of a large glass bell. *Maybe he left me alone—plans to leave me alone for good—because he actually fancies Phillipa.*

As she approached Bones and Phillipa, Sarah felt like one of those gray, winged skates she'd observed in the waters of Jamaica on vacations with the earl and Max. Then she'd shrieked away in fear. Now she knew how it felt to skate along the bottom of the ocean. *Lie low,* she counseled herself. *Lie low, lie low. And observe.*

"Hello, Sarah," Phillipa practically hissed as she finally came too close to the chattering pair to be ignored. "How fascinating to see you here."

"How fascinating that you chose that skirt this morning," Sarah murmured, barely missing a beat. As Phillipa glanced wildly down at her hindquarters, Sarah established herself next to Bones. "Hey, stranger," she said.

With the orderly motion of a clock Bones switched his arm around to a half arc over Sarah. *You're not gay!* her thoughts chorused joyously, thrilling at her proximity to Bones's standard rugby jersey. *You're just—undecided!*

Or irritatingly diplomatic, she added, greeting Bones's frankly friendly smile with one of her own.

"Hey," Bones said, knocking gently against Sarah's arms. "What's happening, light of my life?"

"What's happening is that the Stalker has landed," Phillipa muttered under her breath.

Sarah chose to ignore Phillipa's dig, staring all the more intently into Bones's bluer-than-blue irises. "Not much," she finally drawled. "Getting ready for the big shindig, that's all."

As Sarah had hoped, Bones's eyes lit up—he loved gossip. "Oh, the big wedding, huh?" he breathed.

"You bet," Sarah said, wondering how long she could keep him interested in the latest from Niles Neesly and Company. Long enough for Phillipa to stalk off in despair, hopefully. "You'll never guess what happened yesterday," she began, ready to launch into the tale of Elizabeth's narrow escape at the claws of Lavinia the day before.

"Bones!" Phillipa suddenly broke in. "You haven't met Brandon, have you?"

Suddenly Sarah was facing the back of Bones's jersey, and Bones was shaking hands with a dog-faced bloke Sarah had never seen before.

"Brandon," the unwanted intruder was saying. "Brandon Close, of Memphis, Tennessee."

"Isn't his accent just *darling?*" Phillipa was screeching, like some rare variety of seabird. "Isn't his accent just *the limit?*"

You're the only thing around here that's the limit, Phillipa, Sarah thought in agony. How was she going to get Bones's attention back now?

She'd have to run off to class in a second.

"Brandon's one of those few Americans who actually knows what he's doing in a scrum," Philippa continued breathlessly—deliriously glad, Sarah knew, to have Bones's attention back for a second, even if it was directed only at an acquaintance.

"You on the team?" Brandon was asking Bones, in the mysteriously dull American way.

"No," Bones responded, laughing, clapping Brandon on the back. "No, no, my friend. Just sporting the colors." He gestured needlessly to his Manchester United soccer shirt.

Maybe he really is gay, Sarah thought, losing all the faint tendrils of hope that had gathered in the time Bones had made a half arc over her admittedly idiotically-in-love head. *I mean, he's at least as stuck on Brandon as he was on Phillipa and me.*

Luckily another girl appeared out of the woodwork to quell all of Sarah's fears. "Brandon," Maura McDermott, a sleek, raven-haired freshman cooed. Within a second she was under the proudly exclusive arm of Brandon, sharing a light hello kiss.

Sarah watched Bones's eyes closely for any signs of jealousy. There were none, she was relieved to determine. Instead Bones's eyes danced with mischief—and a bit of gentlemanly understanding.

"Make hay while the sun shines, eh, Brandon?" Bones laughed.

Brandon extracted himself briefly from his rule-Britannia lip lock. "Uh-huh," he said, immediately diving back for more.

Bones turned to Sarah and elbowed her. Phillipa, Sarah realized, had slunk off into the shadows—sure she was beaten? Sarah wondered. Or sick of trying?

"Yanks," Bones said.

"Yack," Sarah answered, unable to stop wisecracking in the face of her complete confusion.

Bones laughed. "Are you free for lunch?" he asked, linking his arm in hers.

Sarah laughed back—completely knocked out, as she always was, by the merest physical contact with the boy she adored.

I'm free for whatever you want, Sarah thought as they stepped out into the cold December sunlight. *But what is it—exactly—that you want?*

Elizabeth and Vanessa faced the task ahead of them with all the relish of swimmers preparing to enter a white-capped ocean in the middle of February. "Just grit your teeth," Vanessa muttered to Elizabeth as they opened the mirrored French doors to the large ballroom that served as the temporary holding cell for all things matrimonial. "Just grit your teeth and it'll soon be over."

Elizabeth wasn't so sure. She knew that like the

Sahara, the afternoon stretched before them, insufferable and relentless. "If you say so," she murmured back as they approached Niles Neesly, seated on one of the gilt chairs he had appropriated from the living room for his exclusive use.

Ever since the wedding had swung terribly into view, Mary had appropriated Vanessa and Elizabeth as her two right-hand men—*Like the food tasters that had to sample the pot roast to make sure the king wasn't poisoned,* Elizabeth thought sourly. It wasn't that Elizabeth didn't appreciate Mary's efforts on her behalf that morning—she had. Still, nothing, really, short of six million pounds and a night hanging out with the Wallflowers, could make up for a half hour spent in the scorpionlike presence of Niles Neesly.

"Girls," Niles said, opening up his smile like a deck of playing cards—but not without glancing swiftly at his watch to make sure they were on time, Elizabeth noted. "How lovely to see you again."

Vanessa murmured something inscrutable—Elizabeth was sure it was something along the lines of, *Rot in hell, you sickening dope.* Elizabeth simply smiled—it was all she could tolerate. *If I'm going to have to spend my afternoon in the presence of Niles Neesly,* she coached herself, *I'm going to have to save my energy.*

"Well," Niles said, beaming at Elizabeth and

78

Vanessa as if they had engineered the sunrise instead of simply sitting down in the metal folding chairs that were assembled, pewlike, in front of Niles's gilt universe.

Probably only Lavinia, Elizabeth thought with a flash of something like fury, *is invited to sit with Niles alongside him in one of the gold chairs.*

Like she even waits for an invitation, Elizabeth added.

"You've got quite a job ahead of you, and don't say I didn't tell you!" Niles chortled with glee. Elizabeth wanted to strangle him right then and there, and she knew that Vanessa's beatific smile could only hide an equally murderous urge. "We've got servers to train, and I expect you girls to transmit the standards of Pennington House to our new staff as if your very lives depended on it!"

And what are those standards, exactly? Elizabeth thought. *Marrying someone you don't love? Or—lest we forget—mastering the art of saying, "That will be all"?*

"Yes, as if your very lives depended on it," Niles repeated. He had risen and walked over to the table and was now stroking one of the spoon settings as if it were a very snooty cat. Vanessa snorted, then tried to cover it with a cough. Niles turned around and widened his eyes at Vanessa—if he had fur, Elizabeth knew, she and Vanessa would be able to see his hackles rising.

"Why don't you girls join me over here." Niles coughed. Vanessa and Elizabeth exchanged silent, invisible moues of sympathy with each other, then headed over to the lair of the troll.

"Let's begin," said Niles, smiling in a way that made him look far, far too close to Hannibal Lecter for Elizabeth's taste—especially since they were standing by a fully laid table stocked well with all kinds of knives.

For the next half hour Elizabeth and Vanessa were completely at Niles Neesly's mercy. First he schooled them in the number of guests per table (fourteen—didn't he think they could count? Elizabeth wondered). Then the number of knives: three. Spoons? Four. Forks? Five—Lavinia was having some complicated oyster-and-crab course that required as much metal as a neurosurgeon's tray.

Next Niles quizzed them on the use of each of the forks, spoons, knives, plates, and bowls. Vanessa rattled them off like she was being asked to spell her name, but Elizabeth—although she had gotten used to the earl's predilection for "finger bowls" spiked with mint and tulip leaves to dip his fingers in after dinner—goofed on a few of the more important settings.

"Salad?" she asked uncertainly, while Vanessa silently shook her head and Niles looked like he was going to fling the plate straight at her neck, Xena-warrior-princess style.

"Does *this* look like it could hold more than three tendrils of radicchio?" Niles raged. "Perhaps you should tell our esteemed chef, Baldo Lucchesi, that you'd like him to serve everything in miniature!"

This time both Vanessa and Elizabeth couldn't help rolling their eyes simultaneously. Ever since Niles had secured the hottest chef in all of Europe from his sinecure in Sicily, everything had been Baldo Lucchesi, Baldo Lucchesi, Baldo Lucchesi. You would think Lavinia was marrying the chef and not Max, Elizabeth thought with amusement. Suddenly her eyes filled with tears. *If only she were,* she thought. *Then Max and I could be together, no problem.*

Niles drew an immaculately ironed and mono-grammed handkerchief out of his vest pocket and patted Elizabeth on the arm as he handed it to her. "There, there," he murmured. "I know what high standards you girls hold yourselves to." Niles pronounced *girls* like *gulls.* Elizabeth took the handkerchief and politely dabbed at her eyes, handing it back to him with a little deliberate frown to keep herself from laughing. The thought of her getting teary over place settings when she had so much more to worry about was so hilarious that it had dispelled her misery on the spot.

Niles looked at his watch and jumped. "Oh! I must fly," he trilled. "A wedding planner's work, you know. Good luck!" Using the handkerchief Elizabeth had crumpled like a kind of flag, he gave them a triumphant wave and headed off.

Elizabeth and Vanessa could already hear the servers mustering in the hall, like a battalion. Niles's voice rose above the crowd. "Just go through these doors and Elizabeth and Vanessa will assist you," he called.

"Here we go," Elizabeth said.

"If only we were already gone," Vanessa shot back.

Elizabeth couldn't have agreed more.

Vanessa couldn't have asked for a worse crowd. First, she and Elizabeth had had everyone sit down in a circle and introduce themselves, strictly for the purposes of making the wedding day go as smoothly as possible (no mad shouts of, "You! You over there, with the pink hair!" across the dining hall, thank you very much). It was still practically more than these goons could manage—most of them threw their names out onto the floor like a challenge, smirking all the while.

"Bridgit."

"Pete."

"Olive."

In an attempt to break the ice—*But why did Yanks always feel that they had to break the ice?*

Vanessa wondered—Elizabeth had them go around a second time and explain what they did for a living. Vanessa crossed her arms with exasperation—they worked for the catering company for a living, didn't they?—but soon realized that Elizabeth had picked up on some undercurrent that she hadn't noticed. The responses went around like a bowl of strained peas no one wanted to try, all tossed out even more grudgingly than their names, if that was even possible:

"Documentary filmmaker."

"Dancer."

"Musician."

To her left Vanessa saw Elizabeth tighten up and give a clearly forced but polite smile to the crew of artistes. So that was the problem, was it? The bloody geniuses didn't think much of two girls their ages who appeared to be only—ahem—maids?

"Let's get started," Vanessa said crisply. She'd be damned if she was going to be held hostage to a group of pretentious dunderheads any longer than she had to. "First, let's discuss the menu and the method of serving we prefer at Pennington House."

As Elizabeth read off some of the house rules in her clear voice to the group of drastically scornful twenty-year-olds, it occurred to Vanessa that in a horrible way, it made sense for the group of hired servers to assume that she and Elizabeth might not have too much on the ball—even if it was only a result of their communal desire to distance themselves as much as possible from the actual paying work they had to do. After all, most intelligent twenty somethings who could be doing something else didn't just up and sign themselves over to a life of servitude to the higher classes, did they? Not in the millennium.

Not really since World War II, Vanessa added, musing.

"So let's go over the table service," Elizabeth was concluding.

After Elizabeth split the thirty or so servers in half, they each took one side of the table and began to go down the courses, the orders, how long they'd wait between each course, what a server should do if a guest required special items.

"And, of course, you can always find me or Vanessa if you need to know anything," Elizabeth was telling her group. "But be sure to simply tell the guest 'of course' and take care of the rest of the table as quickly as possible."

"Oh, absolutely," a tall bloke with horn-rimmed glasses said in mock solemnity, turning around to the girl behind him to give a silent look of horror.

Of course it was exceedingly irritating, Vanessa thought for perhaps the eighty-thousandth time, to have to put on the mask of absolute servitude when one was taking care of the very wealthy. But that didn't make Elizabeth or her miniature versions of Mary and Niles. They hated this rot as much as any of these kids, but it was a job, wasn't it? Where did they get off?

"Please pay attention," Vanessa shot toward her group, raising her voice so that the tall boy would know her words were also directed toward him. "We only have time to go over this twice."

"I'm sure we'll be able to remember it," a girl with hennaed hair and catlike eyes said to Vanessa. Vanessa almost whirled around, but she controlled herself. Had there been a hint of sarcasm—and contempt—behind that seemingly agreeable statement?

Just get this over with, V., Vanessa thought. "Good," she said curtly, preparing to again go over all the information that everyone had—hopefully—already digested.

Still, as she ran down duties she had performed thousands of times, a little thought kept teasing her at the corner of her brain. *I know why I'm here. I've got to get all this business settled with the earl before I can begin my real life. That's the only reason I'm not more—involved.*

Vanessa glanced over at Elizabeth's bland, pretty face. *That's right, isn't it?* she thought, feeling—strangely and awfully—that she'd like to have someone to talk it over with. Someone—maybe—like

Elizabeth? *I have to finish my mother's business before I can start my own life, right?* she could ask her. But would Elizabeth know the right answer?

Suddenly Vanessa wondered what Elizabeth was doing here. If the earl and Pennington House weren't a scary chapter in her family's history, she knew she'd be miles away—*Doing what?* some part of her asked, panicking. *Doing something,* she responded. But what was Elizabeth doing here?

She must be like me, Vanessa suddenly realized. *She's intelligent, she's been to university, and she's clearly able to do other things. Something in her past must be—stopping her.*

It was a jarring thought—Vanessa hadn't considered before how her past might actually be "stopping" her. But she wasn't able to pay attention to it for very long. Suddenly the fragile calm of Elizabeth's face broke, and tears began streaming down.

"Sorry," Elizabeth mumbled softly, walking stiffly and quickly toward the door. The French doors slammed behind her. Her group looked after her, and Vanessa thought she could see a hint of triumph in some of their eyes. *We took care of her,* they seemed to be saying.

Vanessa collected herself. Well, that was the kind of thing that happened if you thought about things too much—you left yourself open to things.

You lost control. You embarrassed yourself. You gave up all of your power.

She was never going to let anything like that happen to her.

She turned to the group of beady-eyed waiters. She felt a welling up of rage. *If you only knew,* she wanted to say to them, *how little you had to do with what just happened here, you little ingrates.*

But she said nothing of the kind. "Well," Vanessa said, grateful for her incredible wealth of English reserve. She'd just act like nothing had happened—just like she always did. And put these brats to work. "Who wants to go over all of the place settings again? You're all going to have to do it, you know, so let's have some volunteers. I don't have all day."

Max walked back and forth in the hallway in front of his father's office like a guard. *This is ridiculous,* he told himself. *Just put your hand to the door. And knock on it.*

But somehow, however much he pictured his knuckles rising up, the three sharp raps that would be required—he couldn't.

Max had tried to work up the nerve to talk to his father last night, but after picturing the conversation in his head at least thirty-seven times, he still couldn't figure out how to start it. The current version went something like this:

Father, is it true you have an illegitimate child? I have to know because my fiancée is using that information to blackmail me into marrying her.

Knock, knock, indeed! This would make their little chat about Sarah's sex life (and hopefully lack thereof) earlier this year seem like a conversation about Darjeeling versus Earl Grey.

But as he propped himself up by a window to gain whatever small vestiges of courage he still possessed, Max knew it was a conversation they had to have.

This marriage is insupportable, Max thought. *I can't do it. Not to Lavinia—*(for *Lavinia,* his brain appended sarcastically)*—not to Elizabeth, and not to—not to—*

Not to myself, he finally finished.

For that was the final rub. For Max knew that whatever his father had done or hadn't done, it wasn't a burden that his son should carry into the next generation. And it *certainly* wasn't a burden Max should plan the rest of his life around!

Was it?

Sarah's all right, Max thought, desperately trying to convince himself that that was true, that he wasn't being selfish. *She's strong and spunky. If there's a scandal, she can certainly weather it.*

Max rubbed his temples. He knew he didn't believe that—not really. Sarah was young and sensitive, she was an adolescent, and whatever crimes were brought down on his father's head, they would surely fall on hers ten times more, just by virtue of the nature of the society they lived in and her age.

But I can't make that right, Max thought. *I can't change the whole world just to protect my sister. I wish I could—but I can't.*

Admitting his relative powerlessness made Max feel suddenly calm. It was a fleeting feeling, he knew, but that was all the more reason he should act on it—immediately—before it vanished.

If Father's done something, it's his responsibility to make it right, Max thought. Seeing his father blindly delight in Lavinia's evil machinations yesterday at breakfast had suddenly made that eminently clear. Although he couldn't picture his father—his father!—ever having done anything as despicable as fathering a child and then abandoning it, stranger things had happened. He certainly never would have predicted that calm, cool Lavinia would have ever resorted to blackmail just to tie up her title and her hoard of Limoges gravy boats, for instance.

If there are lies that my father has told that have hurt people, Max thought, *I certainly can't make it right by living another one.*

He lifted his arm to knock again. If—as Max hoped—Lavinia's accusation was completely baseless, then he would be freed. He could go back to step one: with his work, with Elizabeth, with the next step of his formerly planned-out, superscheduled existence.

And if Lavinia's story was true—?

Then the man who is responsible will have to deal with the problem, Max thought, surprised at the surge of anger he suddenly felt. *If my father has done wrong, he should correct it.*

That's always what he raised me to do, isn't it? Max thought.

That decided it. Max strode purposefully to his father's office and raised his fist to knock on the door. "Father," he prepared to answer to his father's voice. "It's me. Max."

"Elizabeth!" came out instead.

Like a streak of light, Elizabeth had flown by the door at the end of the hall, running like the devil was chasing her. It *had* been Elizabeth, hadn't it? Max wondered. He had only seen her out of the corner of his eye, and the house was filled with strangers involved in the wedding preparations.

If it was Elizabeth he'd seen, Max was sure she had been crying.

Damn, damn, damn, damn, Max thought. He'd already done so much wrong just in agreeing to this whole stupid thing. He was a cretin. Would Elizabeth ever forgive him? Would he have time enough to undo the things he regretted doing?

"Elizabeth!" Max said, running after the figure. It *was* Elizabeth he saw, in her familiar uniform of khaki pants and a blue shirt. After racing through two archways he finally caught her by the shoulder at the bottom of the stairs.

Elizabeth turned around, saw who it was, and dropped her head. But not before Max could see her tear-streaked face—and her frightened, abject eyes.

"Oh, Max," she said, bursting into tears. She pressed her face to his shirt.

Max didn't know what to do except to put his arms around her. "I'm sorry, I'm sorry, I'm sorry," he murmured, breathing in her familiar scent. Even though she was weeping, he was only glad—glad to have her in his arms again. "Sorry for everything," he said bitterly, looking down at the soft strands of hair pulling out of her ponytail.

Elizabeth raised her face, and Max heard her breath coming in great gulps. "It's not you," he finally could make out. Max felt relief but also confusion. *If it's not me, what is it?* he thought. "It's not you," Elizabeth finally forced out, rubbing her face back and forth on the material of his shirt. She lifted her face again and looked right in his eyes. "It's *everything*," she said.

Well, that cleared that one up. Max drew her close again, then looked around. Once again he and

Elizabeth were gallivanting in the front hall, where the relationship was only in sight of the entire world. "We can't talk here," he said, hoping Elizabeth wouldn't be too angry at still having to hide everything that had passed between them. It wasn't that he was ashamed—couldn't she see that? He was only trying to protect her: from being fired and from Lavinia's very, extremely sharp claws.

Putting his arm around Elizabeth's heaving shoulders, Max drew her quickly up the stairs. He didn't want to bring her to his room—she might think that he had the wrong idea. But there was nowhere else they could be sure of privacy—the garden had served that purpose in the summer, but now it was buried under a few feet of snow. *And I just won't think about how beautiful she is,* Max told himself, remembering that evening he and Elizabeth had spent in his bedroom a month ago more strongly each time he tried to push it down in his mind. *I just won't think about it.*

"It's just too much," Elizabeth sobbed as Max finally settled her in his most comfortable chair, the one he always used to read spy novels—not that he'd been doing much of that lately. He took a tissue from the box Mary always kept neatly in the sitting room and began to gently wipe under Elizabeth's eyes. Although it made Max nearly physically sick to see Elizabeth in such agony (especially when he knew he was the cause of most of it), he also couldn't believe his luck. Here she was! So close to him! And they were talking again—at least, she was talking to him, which was the important thing. It was more than he could have wished for.

"Everything is just way too much," Elizabeth said again, taking the tissue from him. Their hands touched, and an electric shock passed between them. *Just ignore it, man,* Max told himself fervently, withdrawing his hand and making sure to give Elizabeth her personal space.

"What's too much?" he asked gently.

Elizabeth looked at him with exasperation. "What do you think?" she asked, giving him a not so light punch on the arm. "You're marrying Lavinia, and I'm going to be . . . serving you your soft-shelled crabs," she finished, breaking into more sobs.

Max had to stop himself from shouting, *Don't give up yet, Elizabeth! I'm working on it, dammit!* He stopped himself just in time, though—he didn't want to raise her hopes about telling the earl what was going on if he wasn't going to be able to deliver the goods later.

It didn't matter, however—Elizabeth clearly had no such illusions and had rushed ahead. "And I just can't stand being away from my family at Christmastime," she said, bursting into a fresh round of tears. She looked down at her hands, her shoulders shaking. "I know it's stupid. But it's really hard."

Was that all? Max could get her a ticket—he could fly her family in, for God's sake!

"Elizabeth," he began, excited to have something he could do *for* her instead of *to* her for once. "I can—"

But Elizabeth cut him off. "I told you what happened with me and my sister," she said, slowly ripping a tissue into a pile of neat shreds. "I told you why I had to leave California and school and everything."

Something in her tone made Max sit back.

Elizabeth flung the shredded tissue on the floor. "I just can't stop thinking about my family," she said, picking up a fresh tissue and blowing her nose aggressively into it.

Max hid a smile, sitting down on the arm of the chair where he had placed Elizabeth. Even weepy, sobbing, red faced, she was beautiful. She was more than beautiful. She was the woman he loved. "Tell me the whole story again, Elizabeth. From the beginning."

"It's a *really* long story," Elizabeth said, giving Max a warning glance.

Max laughed. He wanted to hear the story again, no matter how long it was. He would never tire of hearing how Elizabeth—beautiful, intelligent, fascinating Elizabeth—had wound up being a maid in his house. Stupid Pennington House.

And thank God she had, or he never would have met her.

"I have all the time in the world," Max said.

As if it hadn't been bad enough being humiliated by Lavinia in front of everyone. As if it hadn't been bad enough spending the morning with Niles Neesly. As if it hadn't been bad enough bursting into tears in front of a bunch of kids who thought she was too stupid to do anything more than sweep out a grate.

She had to run into Max at her moment of maximum misery.

When Elizabeth had slammed out of the ballroom's doors, she'd had nothing more on her mind than the fresh white pillow on her narrow cot—the pillow she was going to stain with her tears as quickly as she could bury her face in it.

But of course, the man she loved had to be standing directly in her path.

As much as she'd hated it, she'd been grateful to see Max. And desperately relieved that he cared about her enough to talk about her problems with her. For all that she'd tried to bury her feelings for him, they couldn't be held off when they were standing nose to nose. Especially when her waterworks were gushing.

And he hadn't pushed her away, had he? That must mean that he still cared for her the littlest bit, even if it wasn't romantic anymore.

That was something.

Elizabeth allowed herself to be taken up to his room, and she was glad she did, even though Vanessa would have thrown a blue fit if she'd known that Elizabeth had returned to the scene of the original crime. But Elizabeth had no intention of repeating the scene that had happened the last time she'd been alone with Max in his bedroom. She needed a friend now, didn't she? More than anything, she needed a friend.

Still, Elizabeth was horrified to hear the story about Jessica and Sam spilling out of her again like a pot boiling over. "It's a long story," she heard herself warning him. However tangled all the threads were in her head now.

Max merely crossed his arms and looked amused. "I have all the time in the world," he said.

Elizabeth's anger flared briefly. *You'd better— with all the trouble you've caused me!* she wanted to cry. But she didn't. She was equally to blame—if not more so—for all that had happened between them.

"You know I have a twin, Jessica," Elizabeth said. Max nodded slowly. She couldn't remember if she'd actually ever told him that. But it didn't matter now.

"Before I left California, I had a boyfriend, Sam," Elizabeth began.

Elizabeth could feel Max stiffen immediately. She drew back in response and looked down at her hands gathered in her lap. Was it because he was jealous? Elizabeth wondered. Or because he thought she was a slut?

Maybe it was both.

Elizabeth was unable to speak for a moment. "You had a boyfriend . . ." Max finally prompted.

Elizabeth took a deep breath, relieved. The way to get this out was as quickly as possible, obviously. "I had a boyfriend. But before I left, I found out he was fooling around with my sister."

Elizabeth forced herself to look up, worried that Max would have a look of disgust on his face. Well, it did sound like something from *The Ricki Lake Show*. But Max's face was completely impassive. Thankfully.

That gave Elizabeth the courage she needed to continue. "We were in a motel," she began. "On a road trip. I saw them right outside our room, saw them—"

Again she found herself plunged into silence. This time Max waited a bit to prompt her.

"And saw . . . what?" Max asked.

Elizabeth knew that Max wanted her to feel comfortable telling the story, as though there was nothing overly risqué to report. In a way, there wasn't. But, it caused her so much pain just to think about the kiss alone, on her own time. She'd had no idea how raw her feelings would become trying to explain the situation to someone else. "Saw them : . . kissing very passionately," she said, her stomach still twisting painfully at the memory.

Strangely, Elizabeth found that she wasn't crying anymore. She was all cried out on this subject, apparently. *Well, I've certainly cried enough about it over the last six months,* she thought. *Enough to keep a small craft afloat.*

Max, still sitting on the edge of his chair, didn't say anything immediately either. He looked instead like he was deep in thought. *He better not be thinking about his stupid flower arrangements,* Elizabeth thought. *Because if he is, I will feel free to serve him his dinner from the left—right on to the left side of his head.*

When Max spoke, it was only to ask a question. "Has, um, Jessica ever done, er—this type of thing before?" Max asked.

Elizabeth gave a small shudder. Now Max was going to think she had some nymphomaniac sister! Well, that wasn't completely far from the truth. But heretofore, Jessica had confined her conquests to football captains and pretty playboys and left the moody, ruminative freaks to her far more patient sister.

"No," Elizabeth said acidly, unable to keep replaying her hand pushing open that terrible cheap motel door, revealing a scene she kept wishing she could x completely out of her memory like a line of misspelled type. "No, of course not. I mean, we really go for completely different types. It's not like we haven't overlapped a couple of times, but we've never—done anything like this to each other." She shook her head. "At least, I hope not."

Max crossed his arms again. "Well, do you know how far it had gone?" he asked. "This Jessica-and-Sam thing?"

Elizabeth looked him straight in the eye. What was he getting at—how far did things have to go? Maybe Max was trying to say that sleeping with her hadn't meant much of anything to him either—and since he was getting married in less than a week, that seemed pretty clear. "Far enough," she said, hoping Max would get the point. He winced in response. Evidently he did.

But he didn't stop asking questions. "I may not be making myself clear," Max hazarded, still frowning. "But just reserve judgment and answer my questions for a second." Max smiled a little bit— smiled! Elizabeth was appalled. "I seem to have a sneaking suspicion about something," Max said.

In all their time together Elizabeth had never been irritated with Max, but now she was irritated with him. *What?* she wanted to ask. Unfortunately, at the same time she felt the pull from Max's proximity so strongly that she had to physically stop herself from planting another kiss on his lips. *That Sam and Jessica were secretly given to be married to each other, so Sam couldn't stay with me? Because that's not it.*

And then she wanted to kiss him for a thousand hours.

Elizabeth forced herself to pay attention and not sink into despondency. "A sneaking suspicion about what?" she demanded. Clearly being irritated with him didn't stop her from being wildly attracted to him.

"So you say this was clearly out of character for Jessica?" Max asked, leaning closer and looking her in the eyes.

That brought forth another welling of tears from Elizabeth. This was torture! "Yes," she snuffled, thinking again of that hateful motel bed, its awful green spread. "Except I guess not since I saw it with my own eyes."

"And that's what I find curious," Max muttered, almost too softly for Elizabeth to hear.

Elizabeth couldn't help but let some of the irritation out. "We weren't like some twins, who aren't close. It's safe to say," Elizabeth said, bursting into real tears now, "that we were the most important people to each other."

Elizabeth put her head in her hands and let her feelings go. She felt Max's hands stroking her hair, then handing her a tissue. Elizabeth shook herself to gain control and drew back, concentrating on blowing her nose. Max touching her was much, much too difficult for her to deal with right now.

Because she didn't want him to stop.

"And how did Jess feel about Sam?" Max asked, jiggling his leg like he always did when he was thinking hard about something.

Elizabeth almost wanted to giggle through her misery. Suddenly Max was sounding like a trial lawyer—or a private eye! Actually, it was kind of cute. But Elizabeth couldn't see that it would get them anywhere—Sam and Jessica hadn't been secret jewel thieves on the run, after all. She glanced at the books lining Max's shelves: *Our Man in Havana, The Third Man, Point of No Return.* Too many mysteries down the hatch, clearly, she thought, getting ready to put her hand up and stop Max's wild speculations.

"Well, obviously she liked him," Elizabeth said, trying to keep the rancor out of her tone.

Max sounded disappointed. "Oh, so you always knew she liked him?" he asked, settling back in his chair.

Don't go! Elizabeth had to stop herself from crying as he went farther away.

Still, *that* thought was so ludicrous, Elizabeth let out a near bark of laughter. "No, not at all," she said, thinking of the contemptuous way both Jessica and Sam had always spoken about each other. God, had they agreed to do that? It was all so sickening. "I mean, we all lived together for about a year. Jess *hated* Sam, and Sam *hated* Jess. They could barely be in the same room together." Elizabeth sighed and ripped another tissue in two. Now she knew why Jessica had been so angry, didn't she? "She nearly *killed* me when I started going out with him," Elizabeth finished.

Elizabeth felt her mood descending to a nadir. How long had it gone on, then? Had they always been in love and hidden it? When had it started? Was Sam just playing with both of them? Then why had Jessica kept it a secret from her?

"You can see I'm sick of all these triangles," Elizabeth said, blowing her nose more furiously than she really needed to. Max winced again— *Good*, Elizabeth thought.

"Did she ever come around?" Max asked. "I mean, before the kiss. Did she ever seem to like Sam?"

Elizabeth shook her head again, dismayed by what Max was revealing. That's why this was all so painful—her sister and Sam were unbelievably duplicitous! *At least Max admitted he's stuck between me and what he has to do*, Elizabeth thought angrily. *Even if he's just lying to save my feelings.*

"I was having a horrible time," Elizabeth said as calmly as she could manage. "On the trip, that is. Keeping them from ripping each other's throats. Jess never stopped trying to get me to break up with Sam. Never." She was stunned at the thought of her sister turning her—admittedly powerful—manipulations on *her*. *You could have just asked me for him, Jessica!* she wanted to scream across the Atlantic. *That would have been better than this, and it's not like you haven't done that before!*

"Can I ask another question?" Max asked, in a tone such that Elizabeth knew he would go ahead and ask the question whatever she said. Elizabeth shrugged a *whatever* in his direction. Max was clearly going to take this to the finish, whatever it was.

"Did you remember things you should have noticed after you realized they were having a fling?" Max asked.

Mid–nose blow, Elizabeth found herself stumped. She went back through the summer, through the year before, thinking of any notes, any strange looks, any secrets that seemed to have passed through the wrong channels. That was strange—there really weren't any. God, she must have been blinder than she'd known—any idiot always remembered clues that you'd neglected to

103

pick up on after it was revealed someone was having an affair. Score two for Elizabeth being the biggest chump in the world. "No," she said slowly. "Not unless you consider fighting all the time to be a sign of true love."

Max laughed. "Well, I guess it can be, sometimes," he agreed. "But that's a very particular type of love."

"Yes," Elizabeth said, remembering how she and Sam had first dealt with their unmistakable chemistry. It was sparring, but it was also flirting in its own way. And Elizabeth knew that wasn't how it had seemed between Sam and Jessica at all—they had always just seemed to want the other one out of the room as fast as possible. So their facades wouldn't crack? "It *is* a different type of fighting," she agreed. But what did it matter now?

Things changed. They always changed and—lately—not for the better. Elizabeth heaved a sigh and looked up at the ceiling, unwilling to believe what a bummer almost every aspect of her life had become. "It doesn't matter now anyway, does it?" she asked. "I mean, they're together now, and that's what matters."

Again Max looked disappointed. "Oh, they're together, are they?" he asked, sighing with Elizabeth. "Well, I guess that throws my whole theory into the circular file."

Elizabeth looked over at Max. What theory? "Well, I don't actually *know* for a fact that they're together," Elizabeth began. "I mean, I left the country the next day."

Max laughed. "You left the country the next day?" he said. "Wow, you really don't mess around, do you? You should be one of those Mafia kingpins—once you're on the outs with you, you're really on the outs."

Max's face took on a strange look suddenly. Elizabeth wondered if he was wondering the same thing she was. When would they really, finally be on the outs with each other?

And who was going to cut the other one off?

But Max, she could tell, still had some nattering thought about the matter at hand. "So, I am correct in assuming you've never talked to your sister about this?" he asked.

Elizabeth looked at him in exasperation. Why, why, why was she always supposed to make everything better? It was like she had a three-foot-high sign on her forehead, blinking *Sucker*.

"I haven't talked to Sam *or* Jess since leaving America," she said evenly. "My parents were so angry at me for abandoning Jess in the middle of the country, I haven't contacted them either—not ever." Again she felt the shock of how angry they'd been at her at the airport. "They made it clear they weren't very pleased with me," she said regretfully. "I told you that, Max."

She braced herself for the onslaught of Max's criticism. *How could you just abandon your sister, whatever she'd done to you? How could you not speak to your parents for sixth months? How could you tear apart your life over one measly betrayal?*

But the onslaught never came. Instead Max asked a question Elizabeth simply didn't understand. "So you don't really know for sure whether or not you were set up," Max said thoughtfully.

Now Elizabeth was sure Max had cracked the bindings of one too many a spy novel. "Max, what are you talking about?" she asked. "This wasn't a police sting."

But Max wasn't laughing. In fact, he looked like a mad genius holding up a vial of marvelous green stuff that would save the world. "Elizabeth, think about it," he said eagerly. "You don't recall any signs of this affair—it really came out of the blue. Even now nothing has been settled—you don't know that they're together; you don't know anything."

"So?" Elizabeth asked. What was Max getting at? "I can take a hint."

"Exactly," Max said, his eyes shining. He looked like he always looked when discussing literature with Elizabeth. Except this wasn't literature.

This was her life. Now she definitely wanted to stop Max, but she couldn't find the energy to interrupt him. Probably she wouldn't have been able to anyway. "Instead of assuming that Jess was being two-faced all this time, doesn't it make sense to assume that this was only the last in a line of attempts Jess was making to break the two of you up?" Max said excitedly.

Elizabeth was shocked into silence. Her first thought, after a long interval, was, *That's too easy.* Her second thought was, *That's the stupidest way of breaking somebody up I've ever heard of.* Her third thought was, *But it worked, didn't it?*

It still left one question open. Had Sam merely been surprised by Jessica's sudden attack of passion? Or had he wholeheartedly endorsed it?

Max had continued, gaining momentum with each new thought. "I mean, Elizabeth, think of it," he babbled. "I might be completely wrong, I know. But from what you've told me about your sister, stealing your guy doesn't seem her style. But showing you that he's just a *jerk* might be."

"Well, she'd be kind of a jerk too!" Elizabeth said with some heat. The events of that night were replaying backward in her mind, like some art-house film.

Max nodded. "Totally. I mean, it's a really stupid method. But she was desperate, right? She'd been trying to show you he's not trustworthy all year? So what's the best way to show you—to really *show* you—that he's the guy she thinks he is, not the guy you want him to be?"

Elizabeth covered her ears—this was all too much for her to take in. "I just don't see how it helps anything. I mean, everything is over anyway. Whether or not Jess did this for some twisted reason or because she was betraying me, it was a horrible thing to do."

Elizabeth thought, with that, the subject would finally be closed—and she would start getting some of the sympathy she needed.

But Max clearly wasn't going to let her off the hook.

"Elizabeth," he said gently. "Don't you think you owe it to yourself to at least find out for sure?"

Max grimaced as he asked the question. This was difficult for Elizabeth, he knew. But he just couldn't reconcile himself to the thought that her sister would have betrayed her. It just didn't fit.

I hope I'm not just feeling this way because I don't believe my father abandoned his own child, Max thought. *I hope I'm not raising Elizabeth's hopes falsely. But I don't believe my father is capable of doing anything like that any more than I can see someone who loved Elizabeth for years and years suddenly throwing it all away on someone she hadn't been able to stand five minutes before.*

"I'll have to think about it," Elizabeth said softly. She looked tired and spent, but at least she was no longer crying.

"Elizabeth," Max said, not knowing why. She looked up, and suddenly they were kissing.

"Oh, Elizabeth," Max said. "I'm so sorry for everything."

"Max," Elizabeth said, between kisses. "Why can't I stay away from you?"

Max took Elizabeth's hands in his own. Well, he was going to make a promise of sorts anyway, even if he couldn't keep it. This was crazy. How was Elizabeth ever going to believe that people would rather die than betray her if people—including himself—kept betraying her out of sheer cowardice?

Max drew Elizabeth close to his chest and kissed the top of her head. "I'm going to try to make sure you don't have to," he said.

Chapter Five

Elizabeth finished rinsing her face with icy-cold water, then looked up in the mirror.

The same old face she'd been seeing for the past six months stared back at her.

Still, a hint of a smile crept across her face. "There you go," Elizabeth said softly to herself, in case anyone was wandering around outside the bathroom door. "Go ahead. Smile."

Unburdening herself to Max had made Elizabeth feel like a terrible yoke had been taken from her shoulders. For the first time in months she felt—relatively—calm and collected.

"Don't freak, Wakefield," Elizabeth muttered, rubbing her face dry with the scabby, thin towels that—surprise!—somehow always managed to make their way upstairs to where the help lived. "Just enjoy the moment."

Could what Max had said be at all true? Could Jessica have really staged that whole thing just to make sure she broke up with Sam?

Elizabeth sat down on her bed and looked at her red-rimmed nails. (Hard labor certainly wasn't great for how your hands looked, Elizabeth had often reflected. Thankfully, she'd never gone in for the French-tips-and-talons bit.)

The facts were as follows. On the one hand, Elizabeth knew what she'd seen with her own eyes. *I mean, Sam and Jess were definitely sucking face,* she thought. *That I'm sure of.*

But as she kept thinking, Elizabeth knew it was the only thing she was definitely sure of. There had been no notes uncovered, no *Oprah* "Aha!" moment, no reanalysis of some significant look between Jessica and Sam that she'd simply passed off as nothing at the time.

And in favor of Max's theory were the following facts: Jessica might be competitive—wildly *competitive,* Elizabeth thought, allowing a trace of a smile to pass across her features at the thought of some of her sister's former antics—but she had certainly never, never (at least, not as far as Elizabeth knew), *ever* taken it into her head to steal one of Elizabeth's actual boyfriends.

In fact, she'd thought most of Elizabeth's boyfriends were *boring, loser jerks,* as Elizabeth had told Max—and as she'd certainly told Elizabeth to her face on occasions too numerous to count.

And she'd hated Sam most of all, Elizabeth reflected. Besides the fact that he was a noisy, slobby, frequently irritating roommate—with that estimate Elizabeth heartily agreed—she'd had severe doubts about Sam's ability to make Elizabeth happy. *He's not good enough for you, Elizabeth,* Elizabeth heard, an echo that persisted in her mind just as in the past—it was Jessica's favorite refrain for months; Jessica had been a broken record on that point. *He's too limited to be a good boyfriend. I'm worried he's just going to take your love and throw it away. Maybe even cheat on you.*

Elizabeth gave a violent shiver at the memory.

Was this how Jessica had finally decided to deal with something she feared—or something she *knew*?

Elizabeth had to admit that it almost— almost!—made sense that if Elizabeth wouldn't admit that Sam was a bad boyfriend, the best way for Jessica to finally prove it ineluctably was to offer herself up as proof.

Still, that was a completely ridiculous thing to do! Elizabeth thought angrily, still so agitated by the thought that her sister might have been just proving a point that she had to get up and walk around the ten-by-thirteen room. *How did she think I wasn't going to believe that she had—self-serving motivations?*

The question practically answered herself. *Because she's your sister,* Elizabeth thought, unwillingly believing the words at the same time she was afraid to believe them. *And you know her. And you know she would* never *do anything like that—not about something this important.*

Elizabeth shook her head again and crossed her arms tightly across her chest, trying to calm down. It was too hard to think about Jessica this new way—Elizabeth had too much hope invested in it. What if she allowed herself to think that Jessica hadn't really betrayed her—and then she turned out to be wrong?

What if Max is only spinning me along for some reason of his own? Elizabeth thought. *What if I returned to California and Jessica and Max were living together in the condo, sharing coffee in the morning and playing footsie under the table?*

Sam, I mean, Elizabeth thought, annoyed with herself. *Only I could leave one triangle with a blonde and an M-a-x and find myself in another triangle with another blonde and an S-a-m. I mean, their names are practically the same—they have two of the same three letters.*

Well, two out of three ain't bad.

Elizabeth shivered again in disgust. The Greeks

had been right—try to escape your past and it will reach out and drop you right back where you started.

Turning away from the window, Elizabeth reached under the bed to the small footlocker where she kept her old journals and the few things she brought from home.

Shaking as if it was very cold—it wasn't—Elizabeth reached for the old brown journal she hadn't touched since she'd come to England. In fact, she hadn't had a reason to touch it in years.

As she pulled open the pages, a cloud of dust fell onto her lap. This was an old book—an old memory book she'd made in eighth grade, one she always took with her everywhere.

Elizabeth had to hold her breath to keep from crying. There was a picture of Jessica, wearing some crazy earrings she'd made herself and way too much makeup. Todd Wilkins! Old pictures of Todd! God, he looked so young and skinny—a total geek, just like Jessica had always said. She turned another page.

Mom and Dad.

Elizabeth lingered on the page for a long time. There were her parents, posing in front of the barbecue at one of Jessica and Elizabeth's birthday parties. It was sixth or seventh grade, Elizabeth knew, but that didn't matter. All that mattered were how young and happy her parents looked—how young and happy *all* of them looked.

Elizabeth closed the book with a snap. Tears were running freely down her face. She sat back and let them come.

When they'd finally tapered off—*As much as they're likely to do for this fifteen-minute interval,* Elizabeth thought sarcastically—she sighed and pulled out the footlocker to replace the old picture book.

A photo drifted to the floor. Elizabeth tried to catch it, failed, and then was shocked into tears again by the image.

She and Jessica were standing on a lawn somewhere—*Our lawn at home, probably,* Elizabeth thought. She and Jessica were chubby, with matching bowl haircuts. They had matching sandals and matching dimples. One had her two-year-old arm wrapped firmly around the other one. *I can't tell which one of us is which,* Elizabeth thought, amused.

The thought went off like a bomb in Elizabeth's brain.

Could *that* be the explanation?

Maybe neither Jessica nor Sam had been doing anything wrong. Maybe Jessica was staging the kiss for the benefit of her sister, who refused to admit that her boyfriend was a cheating dope. And meanwhile maybe Sam was—briefly, at least—under the impression that he was kissing . . . his girlfriend.

Elizabeth continued to look at the photo.

I can't tell which one is which.

Immediately a clamor of dismay rose up in Elizabeth's brain. *You're just fishing,* she told herself. *You just can't stand the fact that both your boyfriend and your sister were fooling around behind your back, so you're grasping at anything that anyone throws you. You know what happened, Elizabeth. Admit it. You really do know what happened.*

Or maybe you're too scared to find out, another part of Elizabeth responded.

It was true that she knew nothing for sure. She'd bolted out of that motel like it was going to blow up like a grenade—and at the time she wouldn't have minded if both Jessica and Sam had perished in the flames. Then, before you could say, "Cheerio!" and bite into a scone, she'd been on a plane bound for London, leaving behind all of the people who'd suddenly become strangers to her.

"I don't know anything," Elizabeth said aloud. "Max is right. I really don't know yet what exactly—if anything—happened between Sam and my sister."

It was Christmas, after all, wasn't it? And soon after that, New Year's. The season of new beginnings. The season of forgiving.

Max's words echoed in her mind:

Don't you think that you owe it to yourself to find out for sure?

Twenty-one-year-old James Leer pulled his Alfa Romeo to a careening stop on the gravel of Pennington House.

Damn! Well, that's what happened when he was thinking too much about Vanessa, wasn't it?

James had given up on giving up on Miss Vanessa. Now that he knew Max was equally gone on a maid, he'd decided he was going to use the time he had left before graduation from Oxford to hang around as much as possible. After all, Max was his friend, wasn't he? And being as close to Vanessa as he could possibly manage couldn't hurt. After all this time she still hadn't given him a real "No!" for an answer.

Until she did, he was going to try to remind her that where he wanted to be was at her side. Until she decided that that was where she wanted him to be too.

Although it doesn't look like Elizabeth and Max went anywhere, does it? James thought, stroking his chin thoughtfully while he regarded the Christmas-cum-wedding decorations that bedecked the front of Pennington House. He wanted to make sure he spent as much time with his best friend as possible before the fatal blow was dealt.

I know Max doesn't love Lavinia. And I know that he *knows that he doesn't love Lavinia,* James mused as he walked up the front steps and rang the great, hollow bell that would summon some servant from the depths of the enormous home. *I hope he knows what he's doing,* James thought, blowing on his hands and being careful not to slip on the slick ice that covered the steps despite some yardman's best efforts. *I'm just glad I'm not the one who's getting married on Sunday.*

Unless it was to Vanessa, of course, James added, restraining himself from laughing at how absolutely much that was not going to happen. *Because you know I'd be there an hour early, with bells tied on.*

The door swung open. Behind it, black haired, brown eyed, pale skinned, and frighteningly lovely, stood Vanessa.

James almost gasped. As many times as he'd hoped that Vanessa would be there as the great doors of Pennington House pulled impressively inward, it often hadn't been her. And now—!

Characteristically, Vanessa said nothing. If anything, James noted, her eyes seemed even more dull and unseeing—she could have been looking out onto an empty stoop.

Well, he wasn't going to let a little bit of frigidity stop him, was he? He'd weathered Vanessa's

119

absolutely arctic blasts before. This was nothing.

"Good afternoon, Vanessa," James said, trying to keep the deep thrill he was experiencing at her mere presence out of his voice as much as possible. He'd be neutral and friendly, and maybe they could have a little talk before she disappeared to wherever she always disappeared to. He walked into the foyer uninvited, then pulled his unused gloves out of his pocket. *You should have been wearing these, you doofus!* he thought immediately. It was imperative that Vanessa realize he wasn't trying to get her to take his coat—he was just laughing at himself. He waved the gloves around, then shoved the gloves back in his pocket as Vanessa continued to stare at him blankly.

"Good afternoon," she finally answered, looking at some faraway spot to the left of his right earlobe.

Before James could provoke another sentence out of the beautiful marble statue in front of him, their heads both swung around. Elizabeth was walking down the stairs—the front stairs, the ones that even James knew that servants weren't supposed to use. Not that he cared, but—

What was happening?

"Hey," Elizabeth said, as if they were all hanging out on a blanket on the beach or whatever you did in California. She rested her elbow for a moment on the banister and looked at them quizzically. A small smile crept across her face.

"You guys are standing under the mistletoe," she said softly.

Vanessa turned around. She was absolutely going to *murder* Elizabeth.

When James had first appeared in the doorway, Vanessa had been horrified by her immediate impulse.

To tell James everything.

It would be a relief, wouldn't it? After all, he knew about the law. Even if he didn't, he knew people who would know. Who could help her out, who could give her advice. And he was infatuated with her, wasn't he? He would want to work very hard to help her.

But for what in return, Vanessa? her brain returned, absolutely seething.

In a split second Vanessa gave over to that greater wisdom. James might want to help her, but he would only be out for all he could get, wouldn't he? And when he'd gotten it—why, then, he'd be gone.

That was the way they all were.

So Vanessa pretended that James wasn't even there. She answered his "good afternoon" dutifully, but only the way she would anyone. The way she would return that answer to the five billion people that were going to tramp through these doors next Sunday on their way to watch the happy couple secure the monarchy.

Why, she was only practicing.

But now Elizabeth had ruined everything! Vanessa was sure that she had managed to be so steely that James would simply retreat into Max's rooms as per usual, his tail held meekly between his legs—so the two of them could laugh and talk about how much they were getting out of the servant girls, most likely. But Elizabeth was laughing—*And what does that girl have to laugh about, may I ask?* Vanessa thought. And James looked like someone had placed a flaming fig pudding in front of him and asked him to choose the first slice.

"So we are," James murmured, glancing up at the—damned—dangling sprig of mistletoe that Mary had tacked up above the front doors.

Damn and damn.

Vanessa was about to make a break for it when James suddenly grabbed her by the shoulders. "So we are," he said again, looking at her intently.

Vanessa wanted to squirm, to push him away or stamp on his foot, but suddenly, it seemed, her arms and legs were no longer connected to her body. *Get off of me,* Vanessa's insides screamed.

And then James's lips were on hers.

The minute James kissed her, Vanessa realized

that this was the moment she had been waiting for since the first day they had met. *Don't stop,* she was thinking as their lips hungrily sought each other's out. *Don't ever stop.*

Then, just as suddenly as it had started, it was over, and James stood before her, panting slightly.

Vanessa felt like a flame had erupted at her feet and was spreading up her entire body. She knew that if she were an honorable girl, she would be slapping James at this moment—she would have yelled, *How dare you!*

She never would have let him kiss her in the first place.

"Vanessa," James began, taking her hand.

Suddenly all of Vanessa's limbs flew into motion. She slapped his hand away and ran up the steps, brushing past Elizabeth—and none too gently, mind you. Before she knew it, she was alone in her room with the door slammed behind her, her breathing coming in great ragged gasps.

What had James been about to say?

Vanessa didn't care. She surveyed the room—the three cots, the three trunks, all their scant, forgettable possessions.

She gave a harsh laugh. Why, she'd thought she was so high and mighty! She thought she was better than Elizabeth! No one, she had told herself, would ever touch her, would ever make her weak.

Vanessa scanned the room again wildly, not even knowing what she was looking for.

I'm just like my mother, she realized. *I'm just my mother, all over again.*

And everything that happened to her is going to happen to me.

Unless I'm strong.

Max's first thought was that James looked like a prisoner being led to the rack.

"God, man," James exclaimed. "You look like hell!"

For a second Max thought the words had come from his own mouth—after all, it was exactly what he had been about to say to James. About James, of course.

Max glanced at himself in the mirror that hung over his bureau, then decided he was better off not looking on the whole. "You don't look so great yourself," he said wearily.

James made a funny face like he was a goldfish, then pulled out his pockets so the white insides were visibly empty. "I'm all out," he finally exhaled.

Max leaned back. If he himself had to suffer, at least he wouldn't have to suffer alone. "What's happening?" he asked.

James sat on the edge of Max's chair and began fiddling around with the standing globe that the earl had handed down to Max when he was eight. "Just another encounter with the ravishing Vanessa, that's all," James said enigmatically.

Max raised his eyebrow. Look at the two of them—in love with the maids! It was ridiculous. "And did she ravish you?" he asked impishly, trying to cover the distress he was feeling in every part of his body.

Instead of laughing, James looked straight at Max. He smiled, then tried to hide the smile.

"What?" Max asked, leaning forward in his chair, really and truly interested now. Something was up, and—thank God—it didn't involve him! "What?" he asked, leaning over and giving James's knee a vigorous push.

Now James truly laughed and held up his hands. "Nothing, nothing," he finally said, shaking his head and rubbing at his temples. He leaned back and looked up at the ceiling, the way they both had as teenagers when they were having their first smoke and trying to look nonchalant about it. "We just got caught under the mistletoe, that's all."

For a split second Max feared that James had—somehow—witnessed his indiscretion yesterday and was just pulling his leg about it. But looking at his friend's white, excited face—his absolute dreamlike stance when he spoke the word *Vanessa*—Max realized it had to be true after all. So James had kissed the snooty Vanessa!

"What happened?" Max said in a quieter tone.

James dropped his head and looked at the floor. "Nothing. Well, everything. Like I said, we kissed. And she kissed me back." He gave Max a lopsided grin. "So now I'm more confused than ever."

Max took a deep breath. As much as he wanted to go over every millisecond of the kiss, it was time, he realized, to let James in on everything that was happening with Lavinia. He couldn't—he simply couldn't—go on any longer without getting his best friend's advice.

Or his censure.

"James," Max said, more fiercely than he had meant to. He lowered his tone so that James wouldn't get freaked out. "I have something to tell you."

At Max's words James's stomach fell. It couldn't be what he suspected, could it? That Max had actually—that Max had actually—gotten a girl in trouble?

"It's about my father," Max said.

James heaved a sigh of relief. "Boy, I am glad to hear that!" He laughed at Max. "You've no idea what I thought you were going to say—"

"I know," Max said grimly, cutting him off. "It

126

involves that in a way. It involves Lavinia too."

James was struck into silence. Trying to look thoughtful and not panicked, he edged his chair closer to Max's so that Max would know he had his full attention. Lavinia? And Max's father? He would have preferred the first problem, thank you very much.

Max read James's thoughts in his face. "It's nothing like that," Max said, allowing himself to smile very slightly. "But it is very bad, and I don't know what to do about it."

James couldn't find a comfortable position. He sat up very straight, then slumped back. He put his hand on his chin, then joined both hands on his knee. *Stop fidgeting, man,* he told himself. *Max is going to think you want to run out of the room!*

Which wasn't far from the truth.

Finally James just settled on a medium-upright position, his hands resting loosely in his lap.

Max smiled, then laughed, then shook his head ruefully. "There's no way to say this, so I'm just going to come out and say it," he said. "Lavinia is blackmailing me into marrying her."

James allowed a grin to pass across his features. Was this—a joke? Or an analogy for something? "Max," he said, hoping his friend would come through with the punch line soon. "What are you talking about?"

"Evidently," Max said, enunciating each word very clearly, "my father is the father of an illegitimate child." To James's shocked gaze, Max responded with empty hands spread wide. "No, I don't know who," he said to the unspoken question, "or by whom. But Lavinia"—he heaved out a sigh—"evidently does. Her mother apparently shared the secret before she died, just in case Lavinia should ever need to use it as leverage."

James was too shocked to think. He still waited for Max's smile, for the laugh and the "gotcha!" that would surely follow.

None came.

"Max," he finally sputtered, his head spinning. "What are you going to do?"

Max smiled at this question. "That, my friend," he said heavily, "is what I don't know."

To his surprise, James found himself itching—positively itching—with anger. All the frustration of the past six months that he and Max had suffered had finally found a source. "Well, you can't let her get away with it, man!" he yelled, shocking even himself.

Max looked up wearily. "I'm not sure how I can't," he said, looking to James's eyes far older than both of their years.

James had never suspected that Lavinia could be this cold-blooded, but now that he knew she was, he had no intention of letting his friend be sacrificed to her—*rapacious jaws* were the only words that came to mind. "Stuff it," he said shortly. "Tell Miss Lavinia to stuff it." He smacked his hands, mimicking someone washing his hands, then resorted to another cliché. "Just wash your hands of her," he said decisively.

Max smiled and looked down at his hands again. Clearly James's advice wasn't motivating him the way it was motivating James himself. "And sacrifice my father's career?" Max said. "Everything he's worked for? Destroy his whole life? And my sister's?"

James was discovering that he had a streak of cold-bloodedness too. The answer came out of him as if he were wearing a powdered wig and a long black robe.

"If it's true," James answered shortly, feeling with every fiber of his being the truth of every word he said, "your father sacrificed *himself* the minute he left that child behind."

Chapter Six

Sarah had reached what she considered the breaking point.

She and Victoria had gone over it a thousand times. Bones was not gay. He *definitely* was not gay. So what was the problem?

Her, of course. It must be something with her. And that's why she'd invited Bones over to her house to watch videos, and she'd demanded that Victoria appear an hour before to help her choose an outfit.

As the two girls surveyed Sarah's admittedly well-stocked closet, Sarah felt like Cher in *Clueless*. All she was missing, she thought, was the remote control to spin her thousands of outfits around.

But was any one of them going to be good enough?

"What about this?" Victoria asked, triumphantly

holding up a teeny miniskirt with a zipper down the front that Sarah had snuck by Mary on a long ago shopping trip.

Sarah wrinkled her nose. Honestly—Victoria could be so dense sometimes. "Too long," she replied, shaking her head.

They had already thrown down Sarah's black-market pleather pants, her lizard mini, and her too tight rinse jeans for the same reason. Victoria flung down the skirt with a clear gesture of frustration. "What, then?" she asked, sitting down on the bed in a huff.

Sarah was fingering a tiny top with marabou around the neckline. She was already wearing the jeans she loved—they were sexy, dark denim, and low-slung, and they made her look at least twenty. To that she had added her teeniest, highest strappy heels, like all the models were wearing with their jeans.

Sarah frowned at the shirt—damn! She needed Victoria's support right now, not more unhelpful advice. Not that any of Victoria's advice could really be called "helpful." "But aren't you going to be . . . cold?" Victoria asked, giving the assemblage of strings and a tiny bit of cotton a fearful look.

Sarah gave her best rendition of a wicked smile. "I hope not," she said. "Not if everything goes as planned, that is." And the two girls collapsed on the bed, screaming with laughter.

By the time Bones arrived, Victoria was long gone. Before she had left, however, she had blow-dried Sarah's hair so that it hung around her face like a curtain and applied a thick line of black over her eyes, smudging her lips with the wettest-looking gloss she could find.

"You look hot," Victoria declared.

As she went to answer the door, Sarah felt like a girl in an ad for . . . well, for whatever, nowadays! As long as there was a slow groove playing in the background and a man in a Jaguar outside.

Bones's hired car wasn't quite a Jaguar, but it was close enough. "Hello, *bellissima*," Bones said, letting his eyes go up and down her outfit long enough to satisfy Sarah's fears. *That's more like it,* she thought as Bones went striding into the front hall as if he owned the place, as usual. Father was off buried with some Greek text in his study, and Max was off somewhere too—probably stuck with the stuck-up Lavinia, as usual. The evening was a runway cleared for a smooth landing!

"Hello, dog," Sarah said, borrowing some words from the veejays on MTV. She tugged Bones's elbow. "May I have your coat, please?"

With a mock-submissive smile, Bones handed over his leather jacket.

"Don't switch it, now. I know you people," he said playfully.

"You don't know us well enough," Sarah said, trying to swing her hips like a model as she led him into the entertainment room, tossing the coat onto a chair on her way over.

Victoria had been especially thrilled with the twist that Sarah had thrown into the evening. Since simply watching videos hadn't worked—maybe Bones didn't want to disturb the sanctity of the films? Sarah wondered—she'd decided they'd watch videos *before*, then go to dinner at a pub *after*. "There's no way he can resist you through all that!" Victoria had gushed.

Sarah had nodded grimly. "He better not," she agreed.

Now she and Bones were snuggled neatly onto the stuffy pink couch, watching a series of channels for one second each, Bones having snagged the remote immediately. "Are you *looking* for something?" Sarah finally asked, allowing the full extent of her irritation to show. Bones always found her irritation simply amusing.

Bones looked at her like she was a very small bug. "Exactly," he said, then nudged her so that she almost fell off the couch. Sarah hit him back with one of the small silk pillows that Mary kept shoving everywhere, like they were all insane and the entire house had to be padded.

Which wasn't too far from the truth, actually, Sarah decided.

"So you want to watch the movie?" Bones finally asked after they'd flipped past the screaming vampires, the stain remover, and the ear surgery for the third time.

Sarah gave an exaggerated face of surprise. "Bones! What a great idea!" she said, letting her mouth hang open like she was nearly idiotic. Bones reached over and slowly shut it.

Now just kiss me! Sarah thought at him violently, trying to zap his brain with psychic mind vibes.

They didn't work.

"Thought you'd think so," Bones said happily.

He never bites, Sarah thought, still delighted to merely be looking at how cute he was in his thrift-store jeans and lensless black plastic glasses.

Last Action Hero, or *Last Call to Action,* or *Action Jack* or whatever progressed through its inevitable explosions and car chases. Sarah snuck glances at Bones through the most exciting scenes. He seemed really into the movie, yelling and egging the bad guys on. But on the other hand, he'd seemed to check her out appreciatively at the door, and he'd called her beautiful—albeit in Italian. That must mean something, right?

Maybe I ought to make the first move, Sarah thought, hoping she would crash and burn again. She felt a dash of panic—maybe Bones had *already* made some kind of a first move and she'd

135

missed it! She swallowed. It was *imperative* that she make the first move, she now realized, as soon as possible or all would be lost. *Just a friendly one,* she thought, looking at the clean cut of Bones's left-hand cheekbone.

Scrooching closer to him on the couch, Sarah leaned over and planted a light kiss on Bones's cheek. He turned to her and smiled—*Good.* It had worked. Now maybe he was going to finally *do* something!

But instead of devouring her lips à la Tom Cruise, Bones only opened his mouth and began to talk about how his agent had gotten him onto the set of the actor's last film. "And see, the way they blow things up is they take these huge cans filled with oxygen . . . ," Bones began, smashing all of Sarah's suspended hopes into a messy pile of shards.

Sarah had to physically stop herself from rolling her eyes. God, what was wrong with him? Or was it something wrong with her? If he didn't like her, Sarah wished he'd just say so. It'd be better than this slow torture.

"Then they also make models of the scenes for all the really gruesome close-ups . . . ," Bones was continuing.

Sarah moved back to her place on the couch and stared straight ahead, mumbling, "Um-hmm," and, "Uh-huh," at intervals. A three-year-old would have been able to pinpoint her dismay, Sarah was sure, but Bones didn't seem to even notice.

At least we still have our time in the pub, Sarah thought thankfully. There, if she couldn't get Bones to kiss her, at least she could get him to talk frankly about how he felt about her—because she was certainly going to tell him frankly how she felt about him.

Once and for all, Sarah thought, with a tiny but decisive nod.

Sarah sat through the rest of the movie in relative calm, glad when the last explosion finally rippled through the TV and the credits began to roll up the screen. Finally! Now they could . . . make some sparks on their own, Sarah thought, grinning at the cheesiness of the pun.

"Bones?" she said, turning to him. "Hungry?"

Bones was facing the couch's arm, his head slumped to the side. A light, almost imperceptible snoring came from his general direction.

"Bones?" Sarah asked, peering closer at his delectable cheekbones and exceptionally long black eyelashes.

Bones was asleep.

In addition to the tailspin Max's theory about Jessica's "setup" had thrown her into, Elizabeth was still reeling from Max's last words to her before she'd finally decided she needed to get back to work.

What had he meant by, "I'm going to try to make sure you don't have to"?

Elizabeth looked down at the scattered china at her place setting and tried to think. Was it something positively meaningless, the kind of pretty sentiment you threw out when you were sure that something was pretty much over? Or was it something more meaningful, like, *I'm going to make sure you don't have to leave me by installing you in my own private suite at the Ritz?*

Elizabeth blanched. *God, I really, really hope Max didn't mean that,* she thought. *I've gotten through this thing so far without kicking him in the shins, and I'd really like to end this season without getting thrown out of the game for physically attacking the other players.*

Elizabeth idly dropped the spoon in front of her into her now finished bowl of pea soup. After talking with Max and repairing to her room, she'd finally reappeared, only to have Cook give her a scathing lecture about how Mary was looking for her and that she shouldn't neglect her well-being by skipping meals. Then she'd dumped practically a gallon of soup in front of Elizabeth, added a chopped tomato and some cottage cheese on the side, and stood over Elizabeth with an expression that said that she meant to be sure that Elizabeth ate every crumb of it.

Using considerable effort, Elizabeth had finally managed to finish the rest of the soup (the tomato she had dropped down into the pocket of her apron—she'd remember to move it before the Wednesday wash, she hoped). After that, the cottage cheese was easy. *Just try to imagine that it's mozzarella sticks,* Elizabeth told herself, shoving the last creamy forkfuls into her mouth. She'd never gotten used to the extremely salty, creamy version of cottage cheese they favored over here— it was a far cry from the low-fat skim stuff Jessica always bought and then left rotting in the fridge.

Jess again. Elizabeth sighed. She decided to try and think about only Max for now—not that that was really a happier train of thought, but it was the one she had the best chance of being able to resolve in the near future.

Or could he have meant that he was trying to get out of the marriage with Lavinia? Elizabeth thought, hoping against hope. It was true that he had tried to get out of it once, but Lavinia had turned things back around her way, the shrew. Elizabeth knew that Max was only going through with it now to protect his name and his family. But still, something in her hinted that if he really, really loved her enough, he would never allow himself to marry another woman—he would tell the family exactly where they could put their stupid expectations. She knew that the lack of love wasn't in her.

It had to be somewhere in Max.

But you said you weren't going to think about it that way anymore, Lizzie! Elizabeth cried at herself in frustration. *Remember, you don't really know or understand these people: trying to second-guess their motivations is like trying to second-guess what direction a cloud will blow next.*

Cook took Elizabeth's plates from her, nodding approvingly at how well scraped they were. "Now, you're wanting to get out of 'ere, miss, before Mary returns and takes us all out for a good talking-to, you are," Cook said, smiling diplomatically but in a way that Elizabeth knew she meant business. Elizabeth decided that returning to her room for a while wasn't such a bad idea after all— if only Mary wasn't lurking on the back steps, waiting for her and Vanessa.

This stuff with Max was giving her a positive headache. Elizabeth rubbed her temples and sighed. How strange it was that Max had been able to help her out with the other half of the mess in her life! Now if only she could fly home to Jessica and ask her advice for sorting out the half that included Max.

Elizabeth stopped rubbing her temples. *That's*

what you really want to do now, isn't it? she realized, unconsciously flicking her eyes across the room to the closet, where she knew her simple suitcase was teetering somewhere on top of Vanessa and Alice's things. *It's not just Christmas and being homesick. You want to sort out all this stuff with Jessica so she can go back to being your sister again.*

Elizabeth bit her knuckles in an effort not to cry. There had been way, way too much crying today already.

It was time for action.

Her limbs feeling heavy as wet mops, Elizabeth walked over to the rickety table that served as a small desk for all of them. She looked out the half-moon window onto the grounds of Pennington House.

As usual, they were immensely beautiful, beyond comprehension, practically, for someone who'd grown up with the postage-stamp version of the American lawn. Now winter had covered them in white, adding a stark, muted aspect.

It's time to go home, Elizabeth thought. *It's time to leave all this snow and teatime and enforced matrimony behind and go home.*

Breaking up with Max wouldn't be as hard as Elizabeth was worried it would be—would it? After all, they weren't really *going out* in the first place, obviously. And he'd already broken up with

141

her slowly but surely, hadn't he? Because what else did proceeding with plans for a wedding with another woman mean?

But Elizabeth didn't want to get stuck in another long, tired conversation. She'd do what she was best at instead and let him come and seek her out if he needed to talk.

She'd write him a letter.

Ripping a sheet of blank paper off one of her many pads, Elizabeth tried to do what she always did when she was completely blocked: just let her thoughts go so the words could come. Surprisingly, the letter came out in one huge gush, as if Elizabeth had been working it over for weeks and weeks.

Dear Max, Elizabeth wrote.

First of all, I want to tell you how much I appreciate you talking to me this morning. All your ideas about what might have really happened between Sam and Jess last spring are really making me think, and you might actually be right. Anyway, I know you're definitely right about one thing: I have to go home and find out for sure *what happened before I can put it behind me.*

Now I'm going to say something that's not as easy to get out. While I really appreciate all your advice (and you know *I do, every word of it), in the end, it also makes things harder for me. Because when you act all great and sympathetic, I don't know how to deal with all the stuff that's happened between us.*

It's not that I don't want to be friends, Max. I do. But I really think that with this wedding coming up, it's important for us to put some real distance between each other before that can begin to happen.

I know how I feel about you, and I think I know how you feel about me. We had a great thing together, but you're getting married on Sunday. You're moving forward with your life. And I've been running away from my life for much, much too long.

I guess this letter is my way of saying good-bye.

Elizabeth stopped and chewed on her pen for a minute. Was that way too harsh? That last line seemed like such a cold way to end things somehow. Maybe she should add something else.

Who knows what could have happened between us? she finally added, after much deliberation.

The sign-off was easy. *Love, Elizabeth,* Elizabeth wrote. Her face became hot. Before she could start to cry, she hastily folded the letter and put it into one of the plain envelopes Pennington House used to transmit all kinds of messages.

Before Elizabeth went back to the kitchen to face Mary's wrath, she slipped the envelope under Max's door.

Max found the note about an hour after Elizabeth left it for him.

James was long gone. He had left Max with an unorganized stew of thoughts—confront father? Betray father? Run off to Tahiti?—and weirdly, now that he knew he had the support of his friend, Max felt *more* guilty about his desire to confront the earl and force him to admit to what he'd done, not less.

It must be because I can almost feel how unavoidable it is, Max thought. But what kind of a son was he, Max thought bitterly, if his own father couldn't even count on his support?

He lost that support, Max said to himself, remembering James's words, *the minute he left that child behind.*

True words. True—but harsh. For at least an hour Max had been in the study, fruitlessly trying to distract himself by consuming what seemed like hundreds of novels that he knew deep down he wasn't interested in reading. He blankly watched his cell phone blink up two messages from Lavinia. He flipped through the first twenty pages of another mystery. He heard Sarah enter with a guest—probably that Bones guy—and disappear somewhere into the house. He knew something was over.

Something was over. But what was it?

He saw the tip of the white envelope sticking out of the bottom of his bedroom door all the way from the bottom of the stairs. Taking them two at a time, he jumped up to the landing, not even trying to convince himself this time that it was some missive from Lavinia, who had miraculously realized the error of her ways. He knew it was from Elizabeth.

Please, don't let this be what's over, he thought, picking up the envelope with trembling hands. He opened up the envelope and pulled out the one sheet of thin paper. It was short. It couldn't be *that* bad, could it, if it was that short?

He read the lines slowly, feeling the punch in the gut between the lines almost immediately. When he finished, he crumpled up the envelope and paper and let them fall to the floor, staring blankly at the wall in front of him. Then, slowly, he knelt and retrieved the two scraps, smoothing them out and placing them in his pocket.

He had to find Elizabeth.

Suddenly that search took on all the urgency of an FBI agent attempting to defuse a massive bomb in a public area. His hand hovered above the intercom. Could he call the kitchen and ask Mary—frantically—where Elizabeth was? No, he realized. Not only might he get Elizabeth in trouble (again), the gossip might get back to Lavinia. *Stuff Lavinia,* Max thought angrily, then reminded himself he couldn't do that. *Yet.*

I'll just have to search the whole damn house, Max decided.

Running down the front stairs as if a pack of wolves were chasing him, Max went through the living room, the front room, and the ballroom—briefly and painfully raising Niles Neesly from some terribly important conference he was having with a gray-suited fellow with two bulging tan briefcases at his feet and what appeared to be several fabric samples. "No, nothing! Don't get up!" Max told them hysterically, slamming the door behind him on Niles's raised eyebrow. That was all he needed.

As he ran through the back hallway, which was lined with windows, Max gave a cry of relief at seeing Elizabeth's familiar form, hiking slowly through the snow-covered garden. She was wearing a red hat and red mittens, and even from far away Max could tell that she was deep in thought. Max never had been so glad to see anything in his life.

I was worried that she had jumped on a plane right away for California, Max realized. *That this letter really was good-bye.*

Because if she had done that when her sister had betrayed her, why not to him?

"Elizabeth," Max shouted, bursting out of the French doors at the end of the hall, not caring who heard or saw them. "Elizabeth!"

Elizabeth turned, and her face fell. It absolutely fell, Max realized—there was no getting around it. Well, he would try to see that he never caused it to fall again—if that was humanly possible.

"Elizabeth," Max huffed, finally reaching her. He had forgotten to put on a coat, he realized, and the air was nippy and very cold. Nevertheless, he was sweating in his thin shirt from anxiety.

"Max," Elizabeth said, putting up a warning hand, her disappointed, resigned face now replaced by a sympathetic one. "Like I said in the letter, I really think it's better if we don't see—"

But Max put up a warning hand of his own, cutting her off. *If something's over, by God, let it not be the thing between me and Elizabeth,* he thought.

"I have something to tell you," Max said.

How Max had managed to get her bundled up and off to a pub, Elizabeth didn't know, but he had worked the miracle somehow. In the car he had refused to answer all questions, and they had shot into London in a blur of snow-colored branches and gray, slushy sidewalks. "I'll answer all your questions when we're alone," he said repeatedly, and finally Elizabeth let him be.

I hope he's not just going to tell me that he loves me again, Elizabeth thought miserably, watching all the stone buildings whiz by as if in a dream. *Because even though that's nice to hear, now I know that won't change anything between us.*

Within seconds, it seemed, they were seated at a back table in a nondescript pub, with two pints of Guinness in front of them. Elizabeth reached out and took a sip of hers—true, room-temperature Guinness was one thing she would definitely not be able to get in Sweet Valley, she decided, even though she hadn't really taken to it in England. "So, talk," she finally said to Max's continuing silence.

Max smiled—he actually smiled. "I'm just," he said carefully, "trying to think of a way to say this that won't make you think I'm crazy, that I'm a terrible liar, or that I need a long rest at a spa," he joked.

Elizabeth smiled back faintly. In truth, she wasn't looking forward to whatever Max had to tell her. She'd already said all she needed to say in the letter, hadn't she? And nothing Max could tell her now could change any of that.

If it could, Elizabeth thought, *I'd have heard about it sooner than six days before the wedding.*

"I told you that Lavinia threatened me with something," Max finally blurted out. "Something that could destroy my family. "But it's bad. Really bad. Worse than you could imagine."

There—he had finally said it. It was on the table between them. Now all he had to do was— *Well, explain everything,* Max realized mournfully.

Elizabeth had been in the middle of a sip of

Guinness. Instead of swallowing it neatly, she half choked, forcing Max to come around to her side of the table and slap her firmly on the back a couple of times before it finally went down the right way.

"You all right?" Max asked. "Everything okay?" All the time he was thinking: *Great work. Give the woman you want to marry the shock of her life and kill her before the wedding, why don't you.*

"Argh!" Elizabeth said, reaching across for Max's Guinness and downing half of it in one long swallow. Why she'd chosen his instead of her own, Max didn't know, but he was glad his had imparted the healing touch. *At least my* beer *is helpful,* he thought.

Elizabeth drew a hand across her mouth and looked at Max as if she'd like to throw the beer in his face—and maybe the table too. "Now, Max, say that again," she said menacingly. "What family scandal is she blackmailing you *with?*"

"It's so bad, I can't even bear to repeat it, but I know I have to," Max finished, trying not to make her any angrier than she already looked. "That's why I didn't tell you before. I'd hoped she'd break or confess she'd made it up, but she hasn't."

Elizabeth looked down at the table, up at Max, then at the wall, shaking her head. Finally, after an agonizing interval, she turned back and looked him directly in the eye. "Tell me everything," she said bluntly.

Max was grateful for the invitation—the order. "Yes, yes. Of course," he babbled.

"Right now," Elizabeth clarified.

"Right-o," Max said. "Just give me a second." Turning to the wall, he drained the rest of his Guinness and wiped his mouth. "Here goes."

"Today," Elizabeth clarified still further.

Max took a deep breath. He'd started this, hadn't he? And now he had to finish it. It wasn't so hard either once you got past the earl part.

"It's a long story," Max began.

Elizabeth rolled her eyes and crumpled up the few napkins lying in the middle of the table into a ball. Max got the feeling that Elizabeth wished she could crumple him up the same way.

But she seemed to find an ounce of mercy in her somewhere. "Well, we've already heard a few of those today, haven't we?" Elizabeth said. And gave him a merry smile.

"Lavinia claims that my father had an illegitimate child," Max said.

Elizabeth couldn't believe what she was hearing.

All that stuff about duty and family and honor had been hard enough for a California girl to stomach. Now this whole thing was turning into an episode of *Masterpiece Theatre*.

"Lavinia claims what?" Elizabeth asked, suddenly feeling all the noise of the pub swing back into her ears. When Max had first spoken, she realized, it had receded suddenly, like the silence before a huge clap of thunder.

"Had an illegitimate child?" she asked again, wonderingly. "With who? When? What?"

Max laughed—a little laugh this time, and bitter. "It *is* somewhat hard to picture, isn't it?" he asked.

Elizabeth, who was trying to do just that with very little success, was forced to agree. The earl seemed a bit stiff sometimes, maybe a bit formal, a bit too fond of the words, "That will be all," but fathering an illegitimate child? She could sooner see him claiming to be abducted by aliens—aliens who liked to sing Broadway show tunes and dress up as action figures.

And *stomach* it easier too, Elizabeth realized.

"Max," she said, suddenly seeing him in a whole new light. So that was why he had been so worried these past few weeks—it wasn't only because of their relationship. Weirdly, that made Elizabeth feel better—it meant he wasn't a coward. He was just caught between two impossible situations—his family or his future. "Is it true?" she asked.

Max sighed. "That's what I don't know," he said, and lapsed into silence.

Elizabeth was glad for the respite. She was feeling a kind of humming—an actual *buzzing* in her ears.

It was rage, she realized.

Not rage at the earl. For all that she now felt inextricably intertwined in the threads of the Pennington family, what the earl had done or hadn't done was of no concern to her, and she didn't want it to be. It wasn't at Max either, she realized. She had been angry—*very* angry, she could now admit—at the lame excuse he had first proffered for marrying Lavinia. Duty! Honor! Who thought about those things anymore? And who, even if they did, got married in their names?

Not Max, she was realizing.

But Lavinia—now, that Lavinia was another story altogether. Although Elizabeth had hated her plenty just as the other woman—the other woman who seemed to take great joy in humiliating the other other woman as often as possible and in public—now she could see that Lavinia *was* really and truly a monster, as she had once called her.

And that whatever happened between herself and Max, he couldn't be allowed to marry her—at all costs.

"Do you know," Max was saying urgently,

leaning across the table toward her, "about the recent scandal in Parliament?"

Elizabeth turned back to Max and shook her head slowly. She hadn't heard anything about it.

"There was a member named Clemens," Max continued. "Arthur Clemens. It was found that he had a mistress—that's all, just a mistress, not a teenager or a boy or anything, just another lady living in London. A barrister, actually."

"What happened?" Elizabeth asked, knowing the answer before it came.

"He was stripped of his position," Max said. "And so was the woman. It was covered in the papers for weeks. The woman finally moved to Spain to escape all the coverage, and Mrs. Clemens left Arthur. It's said she took the children, and his family is living in the countryside now somewhere, under an assumed name."

Elizabeth nodded silently, wordless. She didn't know what to say.

"I can't do that to my father," Max whispered.

Elizabeth turned to him and looked him face-on, the hubbub of the pub seeming to fade away in the glare of her gaze.

"Oh, Max, I understand. I do. But I don't see how you can do this to *yourself*," she added.

Max didn't know what to say. He was immensely

relieved, first of all, that Elizabeth believed him at all—after all this time had passed, now that the wedding was almost tomorrow, he had had severe doubts on that point. But now she was responding with sympathy—he *thought*. Could that even be possible at this late date?

"I'm not worried about myself," he finally said, trying to explain the situation in its entirety so that she would see clearly the risk this kind of revelation posed to his family. "But I don't want to be the cause of my father's downfall—why, his life is his career. And Sarah," he continued, groping blindly in the air for his excuses—excuses he had run through in his mind a thousand times but now could barely remember for some reason. "Sarah's just coming into the age when she would make her debut. If something like this happens— why, that'll be the end of her in society." Max snapped his fingers in the air to make his point, as if his thumb were Sarah's neck.

Elizabeth looked serious. "I know," she said, nodding. "I get all that. What I'm trying to tell you is this: if Lavinia is willing to use this against you to get married, what makes you think she won't use it against you to get what she wants forever, for the rest of her natural life?"

Max was dumbfounded. That thought had never occurred to him.

"And *yours,*" Elizabeth said softly.

Max felt like his head had been dunked in a bucket of ice-cold water. He had been dreaming, he realized. What had led him to think that he could control Lavinia's machinations simply by marrying her? Lavinia, of course, but he had his own blindness to blame too. He had been picturing this blackmailing as an unfortunate bump in a long, dusty road whereon he and Lavinia would tread different but amicable paths, keeping up appearances as necessary for their respective families and for their careers. This, he now saw, had just been the ticky-tacky façade his mind had put on the truth to make it more palatable. The truth was, Lavinia was a terrible schemer, and a life with her would be a life at her ruthless mercy—that is, unless both his father and his sister died off suddenly. *But then she'd have children to use against you,* he realized suddenly. Children! He couldn't allow this to happen.

"Elizabeth," he said. "You're completely right."

"Don't you see?" Elizabeth said eagerly. "This isn't about what happens between us—that's another whole issue. This is about *you,*" she said, her eyes gleaming angrily. The anger, Max realized, was for Lavinia, not against him. "If you marry Lavinia, she's going to keep you on a short leash for the rest of your life. A *very short leash,*" she emphasized, in case he had missed the point somewhere along the line.

Max's breathing was coming in very rough gasps. He felt, he realized, like he had just narrowly averted being hit by an omnibus—or rather, that Elizabeth had yanked him out of the careening vehicle's path.

He could barely get air into his lungs.

"Here. Calm down," Elizabeth said, tapping a fork on the table to get his attention. "Waiter!" she yelled across the pub to the shocked bartender. "Some water, please, over here!"

Not for the first time, Max was grateful for her American forthrightness. "Thanks," he gasped when the tepid glass was delivered by the bemused bartender, and drained it in one gulp.

Elizabeth laughed, looking at him with luminous eyes. "Scary, huh?" she said. "But I had the advantage. I guess you didn't get all the *Melrose Place* reruns over here, or you would have recognized a dangerous woman when you saw one."

Max shook his head, still practically unable to speak. "We got them," he finally managed. "I'm just a dunce."

Elizabeth laughed—an open laugh this time, showing all of her beautiful teeth. *You're beautiful,* Max couldn't stop thinking. *And I love you—truly, madly, deeply.*

"But I know a wonderful one when I see her," Max said, his fingers closing over Elizabeth's open palm.

Chapter Seven

Vanessa stared up at the open window of her mother's old apartment in the crumbling tenement building.

When they had lived there together, Vanessa remembered, her mother had hung blue curtains in the kitchen window to hide the dingy, unwashable glass. Over the years the curtains had turned brown—with age and grease and the stain of soot from the nearby factories. After that initial decorative impulse, her mother had never bothered to change the curtains again.

Nor anything else, Vanessa remembered.

Now someone equally optimistic had tried to overcome the neighborhood's squalor with bits of fluff—lace curtains and a pot of some bluish flower. It was like a cheap umbrella against a raging typhoon.

Well, they're trying, at least, Vanessa thought, desperately trying to take some joy in the small pot of blue flowers, so high up against the blackened building and the gray of the sky. *You've got to give them something for that.*

Vanessa hadn't returned to the building in a while. During many of her trips, before her mother's death, she usually only made it a half hour before the ambulance. As her mother's last boyfriend called her more and more frequently to "look after her mother," Vanessa got used to calling the ambulance herself on the way over just so that she could send the two of them away at the same time—her mother in the lorry and the boyfriend to the pub—before she settled down to cleaning up whatever ungodly mess the two of them had generated with their screaming, drunken fight that week.

"You're a good girl," her mother had said once, near the end, as Vanessa tried to prop her up on the couch and give her some water before the boyfriend burst back in the room, screaming with the news of whatever new crime he had imagined for Vanessa's mother that week. "You know that, don't you?"

Vanessa had barely been able to look into her mother's face, she stank so badly of whiskey. "I know it, Mum," she said, before holding the glass up to her mother's lips.

In Vanessa's childhood it had been her mother who had held the glass up to her lips, who had wiped her face with a cool, wet washcloth when she had a fever and tempted her out of her frequent upset stomachs with buttered toast and lukewarm tea. She had tried to be a good mother, Vanessa knew, and she had been, for a while. She had worked two jobs before the drink had got to her.

Mum, Vanessa wanted to cry at the cold, bleak building. *I was a good daughter, wasn't I?*

But Vanessa couldn't do anything of the sort— she'd be carted off in the lorry herself, *tout de suite*. Still, suddenly Vanessa missed her mother so badly, she could barely breathe.

She could ask James for help, she knew. Help against the man who had reduced her mother's short life to such brutal circumstances. And James, good boy that he was, would provide it.

Vanessa's brain gave her its familiar response, so old now that it was practically rote. *But at what cost?* she asked herself, despairing.

Out of the pocket where she'd been keeping it, Vanessa drew the photo of the earl and her mother. They were staring at the sun, laughing blankly at the photographer. Who had taken the picture? Vanessa wondered again. Some wandering beachcomber? Or did someone else know about the earl's secret?

I'm not stupid, Vanessa thought, staring down at

159

the gray, dulled surface of the photo—so like the gray surface of the building where she had grown up, gone from short dresses to shorter miniskirts, and, finally, to whatever uniform they were wearing at her current job. *I know what James will do.*

He'll leave you, Vanessa told herself, hearing the words not in her own voice but in her mother's terrible drunken cackle. *He'll sleep with you, leave you, and run off with some bird from Oxford.*

Vanessa felt a terrible sinking sensation, as if the pavement underneath her feet was about to open up and swallow her into the bowels of the building, where she would live alongside all the other people it had devoured in the intervening years: her mother; her neighbor's two children in a car crash, the lady down the hall whose hacking cough from cigarettes could wake the dead.

I don't need him, Vanessa thought furiously. *I don't need James. I don't even need the earl or my job at Pennington House.* She looked at the photo she held in her hands. *I've got everything I need to destroy the earl right here.*

The question had been pushing harder and harder at the sides of Vanessa's brain in the past weeks, but she still hadn't managed to answer it to her satisfaction.

So what are you waiting for?

*   *   *

Sarah had chosen the pub because it was the least-assuming one she knew—one where all the men lined up at the bar and women laughing and blowing smoke in their faces were more likely to know how to calculate to the three-hundred-and-forty-seventh digit of pi than where Bones's last hit stood on the charts.

Waking up Bones had been easy, thankfully. After she shouted, *"Bones!"* with all her might, hoping it would shatter his stupid, non-kissing-inclined eardrum, he simply rubbed the sleep from his eyes and given Sarah's knee an aggressive shake for a hello. "Ready for din-din, beautiful?" he asked.

"Very ready," Sarah had said, calling Fenwick and giving him imperious directions to the pub, which she had only been to once, with Max, a couple of years ago after a cricket match.

Bones had donned his sunglasses in the car, as he was wont to do. Sarah grinned. "Don't worry," she said, happy to witness one of his few moments of vanity and happier still to be the one who punctured it. "They won't know you from Adam in here."

"Adam?" Bones said quizzically as she pulled him from the car and pushed him through the door. "Who's this Adam fellow, might I ask, Miss Sarah? And has his last album gone double platinum?"

They crashed through the door, laughing. The last people Sarah expected to see sitting in the pub were Max and the blond American maid, Elizabeth.

Sarah was about to utter a cry of recognition and come introduce Bones when Elizabeth looked up and saw her. The look of fear on Elizabeth's face would have shattered glass.

And that was when she saw Max's hand, linked with Elizabeth's, across the table.

"Pig!" Sarah yelled at her brother, surprising even herself and completely silencing all the other patrons in the bar. "You bloody pig!" she yelled again.

"Sarah!" Bones said in alarm, taking her arm as if to drag her away.

Max stood, teetering, Sarah thought, like a cup about to crash on the floor. Finally he crashed and broke.

"Sarah," he said across the pub. His eyes looked as dark as burned-out candle stubs. "Sarah, it's not what you think."

Without waiting another second, Sarah wheeled around and ran out of the pub, into the night.

About half a block later Sarah was surprised to find out that her cheeks were wet. *Well, of course I'm crying,* she snapped at no one. *If Max is cheating on Lavinia, then—*

Then what else is happening? she thought in agony.

Sarah had never thought of herself as someone who depended overly on her brother to set a moral example for the Pennington family. After all, she was the sister who sneaked smokes, who fooled Fenwick into thinking that she was meeting Victoria for a study date when she was actually going to meet Nick and lose her virginity, which thankfully hadn't happened. Anyway, if she wanted to look to a virtuous example, she could always look at her father, widowed young, now happily married to his books and pipe.

But now that Max had been revealed to be as two-faced—*As two-faced as I am,* Sarah finally managed—she felt like the sky had finally fallen and crashed around her feet in blue, icy shards.

I can't trust anyone, Sarah thought, tears leaking out of both sides of her eyes.

Suddenly she felt a hand grasping her shoulder. "Sarah!" Bones gasped, holding her with both arms now that he knew it was her for sure. "I thought I'd lost you!"

Although in truth she had forgotten about Bones completely the moment she'd seen Max holding hands with Elizabeth Bennet, Sarah had never been so glad to see anyone in her life. "Bones!" Sarah cried, grabbing his coat and breaking into a round of fresh tears.

Bones immediately enclosed her in his arms. "There, there," he said, stroking her head thoughtfully. "It can't be all that bad, now, can it?"

Sarah nodded violently into the buttons of his leather jacket. "Yes, it can," she finally gasped up at Bones's chin.

"Now, now," Bones soothed, continuing to stroke her hair. Sarah began to calm down, and her hysteria resolved into a smooth, steady flow of tears.

"It's all horrible," she whispered into his coat.

"I guess some of it is," Bones said thoughtfully. He drew a handkerchief out of his pocket and began to wipe Sarah's tears away as freshly as she produced new ones. "Who *was* that?" he finally asked gently.

Sarah let her jaw drop—Bones had no idea what the problem was, of course! He might even think that was an ex-boyfriend. For a minute Sarah played with the idea of fooling him into thinking that was indeed so, but she was almost too depressed to even speak the truth. "Bones," she said, her jaw beginning to tremble violently again, "that was *Max*."

Bones nodded rapidly, wiping faster. "Let me guess," he said. "That *wasn't* the notorious Lavinia."

Sarah laughed through her tears. "No," she said. "That was the stupid *maid*, Elizabeth Bennet."

"And you didn't know anything was going on between them," Bones said, stroking the space between Sarah's nose and mouth thoughtfully.

Sarah felt her breath coming slower, more calmly. "Well, I knew he had a *crush*," she said with annoyance. "It's not even like I like Lavinia! But it's less than a week before his wedding, Bones!"

Bones nodded thoughtfully. "Your brother doesn't do this kind of thing often, I gather," he said wryly.

Sarah looked up at Bones, his cheekbones standing out sharply under the sallow light of the streetlamp. She still had a massive crush on him, but—really—he was acting awfully thick. "Do *you* know anyone who does?" she said heatedly.

Bones laughed. "Well, not personally, no," he said, moving his hand to her cheek, which he stroked with equal thoughtfulness. "I was just gathering, you know."

Sarah laughed—a real laugh. For some reason, she was feeling pretty calm now.

"That's what I thought," she said, taking his hand. "Let's go get dinner—somewhere else."

Bones put his arm around her and pulled her close. "You took the words right out of my mouth," he said.

Chapter Eight

Max rushed after Sarah, of course, but he found no sign of her or of her male companion on the dark street. After walking around the block four or five times—he'd lost count—searching every dim doorway, he returned to the pub.

"No sign of them," he said, despondent.

Elizabeth pressed her hand against his cheek, then rubbed his shoulder. "You'll explain it to her later," she said, giving Max what he was sure was her best imitation of an optimistic smile. It was enough. They decided to return to Pennington House, with Max cursing himself every block of the ride home.

God, Max kept wondering. *What are the chances of running into Sarah with Elizabeth the very night I decided to leave Lavinia once and for all?*

Well, what were the chances that his perfect mate

would arrive from America, working as a maid in his very own home? What were the chances that his fiancée would then blackmail him into marrying her?

What were the chances that the earl could have fathered an illegitimate child? Max asked himself.

Elizabeth went immediately up to her room when they got home, after giving Max a supportive hug. "You need to talk to me," her eyes said, "but you need to talk to Sarah more." Once again Max was grateful for Elizabeth's amazing ability to be considerate, even in the midst of her own stress—and she had plenty. *She's too good for me,* he thought. *I've got to catch up.* Max fell into a fitful sleep on the couch, waiting up for Sarah.

He didn't wake up until the next morning, coughing into the dry air of the study. Before he'd even gotten a glass of water, he dashed into Sarah's room.

The bed was empty, freshly made and completely flat. Max swore aloud. Did this mean that Sarah had already gone to school? Or that she had never come home at all?

Please, God, let her be at school, Max prayed.

After downing a quick jolt of coffee—he'd found the cup half full from yesterday in his study—Max jumped into his car and gunned his way toward Sarah's school. He wasn't going to wait to see if she got home. Wherever she was, he needed to find her and explain, now.

Your bed wasn't made yet, his conscience pricked him nervously. *Your sitting room wasn't even picked up. So doesn't that mean Sarah definitely didn't come home last night?*

"Let her be safe," he said aloud in the silence of his car. "Let her not have done anything stupid because of me, please."

It was true that the servants—that his lady love! he added ecstatically—didn't always do the bedrooms in order. Sometimes they moved around; sometimes they had other duties that called them away. Right?

When he reached the reassuring, ivy-covered, brick edifice of Sarah's school, Max's breath quickened. Now he would find his sister—and finally truly explain his predicament.

Just let her be there, he asked as he ran up the front steps.

The whole kitchen staff was assembled for the meeting with the famous Baldo Lucchesi.

Or infamous, Elizabeth appended, taking a small sip of her now cold tea. They had been waiting for nearly an hour, but the chef had yet to appear.

His assistant, Vijay Gupta, had been calling breathlessly every half hour. "He's coming up the drive," Vijay finally assured Mary at the fifth call.

"And about time too," Mary muttered as she

hung up the phone and beamed a smile at the waiting kitchen staff. Niles was the only one that responded—with a killer smile of his own and a maximum of fluttering.

"Get ready, girls!" he said breathlessly. "You are about to meet one of the most famous chefs of all time!"

Alice gave Niles a weak smile. Vanessa didn't even attempt to hide her sneer. Elizabeth hid her reaction—tastefully, she hoped—in the dregs of her empty teacup.

Elizabeth couldn't help thinking about Max and their conversation last night. *I was just over him,* Elizabeth thought, both amused and irritated, *and now I'm all bound up in making sure he's not married to Lavinia for a reason that has nothing to do with me!*

Well, Elizabeth reflected, once again dipping into her empty teacup for a respite from the silence at the tense breakfast table, it was actually easier to concentrate on saving Max now that she had nothing to lose in the whole venture.

Because that's really what the problem was, wasn't it? Elizabeth thought. *I couldn't follow along with Max, even though I loved him so much. Because I knew I had too much to lose.*

Did she still have too much to lose, she wondered, now that she knew he hadn't dropped her because he hadn't loved her enough?

Finally the great bell rang. Mary skittered upstairs with Niles close at her heels. Vanessa gave a loud, exaggerated sigh, earning a tsking and a head shake from Cook. Moments later they all appeared, a small, energetic Italian man in tow.

"So!" the man declared. "This is to be the house of the beautiful wedding!"

And that, Elizabeth and the staff slowly realized, was truly the extent of Baldo's English. Everything else that he said was passed through the mouth of Niles, who translated Baldo's musical Italian into the king's English with enviable aplomb.

"Maestro Lucchesi wishes the pants of all the servers to have a sharp crease," Niles declared, looking particularly at Alice, Elizabeth thought—and unfairly at that.

"Maestro Lucchesi is particularly concerned that the soup be served *at the moment* it is dropped into the bowls," Niles said.

"Maestro Lucchesi would wish all of you to have a very happy New Year and Christmas holiday," Niles finally allowed, and Chef Lucchesi placed his beefy forearms on the table. Elizabeth noted with interest that they were incredibly hairy.

Barring the slight physical conundrum presented by the soup request, Elizabeth couldn't see any problem with the chef—despite the fact that

Niles would have to spend the entire evening at his side, translating his demands.

It seemed that Niles was very close to realizing that too. He suddenly looked green at the gills, matching his absolutely grass green silk tie.

Elizabeth felt a small giggle escape, and suddenly Niles, Mary, and "Maestro" Lucchesi were looking at her like she had just fallen asleep at the table.

Guess Lavinia reconsidered Pennington cuisine, Elizabeth thought, and laughed again before returning to the relative safety of the teacup.

James decided it was time to give Vanessa another little visit. It had been nearly a day since he had last seen her, hadn't it? And despite the fact that she had run away afterward, she had responded enthusiastically to his kiss.

She was thawing—finally.

Or else I've just worn down her resistance, James thought, grinning like an idiot.

As usual, Mary answered the front door. "Mr. James," she said, with a slight nod.

As Mary tottered upstairs to try to locate Max—his ostensible reason for visiting—James peeked around the corner of the parlor door, hoping that Vanessa was somewhere in the vicinity.

Luck! James spied around the corner the soles of the graying tennis shoes Vanessa always wore

172

when she had to do really dirty work. Sneaking down the hall, he tried to determine what in the world she was doing.

Her forehead furrowed with concentration, Vanessa was kneeling in the hall, holding a tape measure from one wall to the other. *Must be something for that damn wedding,* James thought, suddenly feeling guilty for not being upstairs with Max, who was almost certainly in the middle of a nervous breakdown by this point. *I'll go upstairs and see him the second I'm finished here,* James promised himself, noting how adorable Vanessa looked as she bit her lower lip and stretched the tape measure against the baseboard to be sure it was perfectly straight.

"Boo," James said, the minute he was inches away from her back.

The tape withdrew with a clatter. "James!" Vanessa said, scrambling to her feet. Her cheeks filled with a deep blush. "What do you mean, scaring the life out of me?" she said, a trace of a smile at the corners of her mouth. She was trying to sound angry, but James could tell her heart wasn't in it.

Feeling a surge of courage, James reached forward and grasped her free hand in his. "What are you doing?" he asked, trying to arch his eyebrow devilishly, a trick he had mastered in high school.

Instead of her normal emotionless mask,

Vanessa seemed . . . almost *nervous*. This was progress! James gave her hand a squeeze, and she actually tittered.

"You're going to cost me my job," Vanessa murmured, and suddenly James swept her up in his arms again.

The Vanessa he had known was not this Vanessa. This was the Vanessa he had always dreamed of: pliant, responsive, her lips warm and eager on his own.

Suddenly she broke away, placing his hands on his chest to push him back. James thought she was going to close down again. *Don't,* he almost said.

"I'm measuring the hallway for the new runner," Vanessa practically whispered, focusing on the buttons on James's shirt. "The old one was two inches too wide."

"Uh-huh," James murmured, sweeping her back into his arms for yet another kiss.

It's finally happened, James thought, feeling the thrill of contact spread over his entire body like a warm shower. *Finally she's opened up to me.*

"James," Vanessa said, breaking off the kiss.

James's breath was ragged. "Uh-huh?" he said, stroking a curl around her left ear.

"We shouldn't do this here," Vanessa hissed, jerking her thumb upstairs, where Mary most likely was rushing around, looking for Max.

Vanessa looked down. "In fact, I'm pretty sure we shouldn't be doing this at all."

Instead of feeling crestfallen, James merely felt restful. Now that he knew for sure that Vanessa had feelings for him, it was up to him to make her understand the extent of his feelings for her. He grasped her chin lightly and brought it up until they were face-to-face. "Hey," he said. "Vanessa. I *love* you. All right? I love you." Vanessa looked quickly down again, and when James brought her face back up to meet his own, he saw two tears sliding slowly down.

"Don't do that," he said softly, brushing the tears away with his knuckles. The tears increased. "Shhh. Shhh."

When Vanessa spoke, her lips were trembling with effort. "It's just that I don't know what that *means,* James," Vanessa finally broke out.

James pulled his handkerchief out of his jeans pocket and began to gently wipe Vanessa's face. She grabbed the handkerchief from him and blew her nose loudly. That broke the tension, and they both laughed.

"It means," James said, after the brief hilarity had subsided, "that whatever you want, whatever you need, I'm here for you." He looked deeply into her eyes so that Vanessa wouldn't miss the seriousness of his point.

"Well, that's all right," Vanessa finally murmured.

"Just all right?" James said, nudging her side with his arm. "You're a cold, cold girl."

Vanessa's dimples showed. "I guess it's a start," she said with a faint sigh. Sure she was joking now, James swept her up in another kiss, and this time Vanessa's arms crept around his neck.

You bet it's a start, James thought, stroking the back of Vanessa's shirt, still unable to believe that he was finally and truly kissing the girl of his dreams. *The best thing I ever started in my entire life.*

Now Vanessa knew why she hadn't exposed the earl.

All this time she'd been desperately trying to convince herself that exposing the earl was precipitate, unwise, that it might entail too much risk. But all the time she'd really been talking about herself and James.

I didn't expose the earl, Vanessa thought with wonder, feeling her still hot cheeks, *because I knew that to do so would hurt James—however indirectly.*

James had left minutes ago, babbling incoherently about his love and securing from Vanessa his right to take her to a movie on Thursday night. Immediately after she had closed the door behind him, her doubts resurfaced like an alligator slowly rising up through the swamp to scan the area for prey. Still, she had no intention of allowing herself to be clamped between his awful jaws today.

I know he might be lying, Vanessa thought. *I know he might disappoint me—he might turn out to be just like that slimy Max. But you know what? I'm old enough to get over disappointment now. And I'm also old enough to protect myself.*

That's what Mum wasn't so good at doing, Vanessa thought sadly.

Visiting the old apartment yesterday had freed something up in her—she didn't know yet what. But whatever it was, it made her aware that she was sick of staying high and above everything, of looking from the outside at other people living life while most of her life revolved around a woman who had been dead for a long, long time.

Momma, I love you, Vanessa thought. *But I'm going to have to let you go.*

Chapter Nine

When Sarah saw Ms. Richards unfold the note from the office assistant and look straight at her, her first thought was that the earl had died.

Ms. Richards was one of the youngest teachers at the Welles School, and she was a favorite among the English majors. With a specialty in French and American literature, Ms. Richards's class was one of the most exciting in school—instead of dumb Thackeray again, Sarah had been thrilled to realize that they were going to read Colette. It didn't hurt, of course, that Emily Richards was a dead ringer for Vanessa Williams, with huge brown eyes and long curly hair spilling past her shoulders—causing a slightly higher male enrollment in her classes than was generally expected.

However, Sarah had been locking major horns with Ms. Richards today, especially after Sarah had exploded at her. "I have things on my mind," Sarah said gruffly when Ms. Richards asked her sharply why she didn't seem to be "with them" today. Out of the corner of her eye she saw Bones and Victoria exchange worried glances.

When Ms. Richards called her to the front of the room and told her, "You're wanted in the office," however, her large eyes were filled with concern. "See me later," she murmured to Sarah, who was too worried to answer.

When she saw Max's long, familiar form leaning on the headmaster's desk, Sarah was too paralyzed with fear to be angry with him. "Is it Dad?" she asked, grasping Max's shirt with both hands.

Max looked shocked—then sheepish. "No, no," he said, taking her hands off his shirt, where Sarah had been doing her best to dig a furrow, and holding them tightly in his own. "Christ, I'm sorry. I didn't mean to scare you. Everything's fine."

Sarah took a step back. She couldn't keep the hysterical pitch out of her voice. "Then what are you doing here?" she screamed, causing the three secretaries to cease their typing and look up.

"Oh, Sarah, I forgot," Max said.

Sarah burst into tears—she couldn't help it. Years ago, when her mum had died, they had informed her in just this way—a sudden note calling her out of class, Max and her father standing grimly in this exact office, everyone looking pained and forbidding.

Max put his arm around her shoulders. "C'mon," he said. "I'm taking you out to lunch."

Out on the street, Sarah shoved Max's arm off her roughly. "Ow," he said, rubbing his elbow.

"I'm still not speaking to you," Sarah said, crossing her arms and striding ahead.

Max kept pace easily and continued rubbing his elbow stoically. "That's all right," he said, piquing Sarah's interest a little. "All you have to do is listen."

When they were finally seated in a small Greek place, with hanging plants in all the windows, that had just opened near the school, Sarah's curiosity finally got the better of her. "So?" she asked, peering over the large, plastic menus featuring tabbouleh and spanakopita. "Are you going to explain your behavior?"

The waitress plunked down two glasses of water. "Yes," Max said, in a more serious voice than Sarah had ever heard him use in a conversation with her. "And I should have explained everything to you before."

About time they started filling me in around here, Sarah thought, more pleased than disgruntled.

"So, I never should have asked Lavinia to marry me in the first place," Max began.

Sarah felt a strange thrill. Max was usually so

formal, so stilted, like their father. It was a relief to hear him finally speak plainly for once.

"Yeah—that seems obvious," Sarah responded, fiddling with her knife and fork, lining them up by their heads, then their feet.

Max sighed. "I asked her," he said, "because Father thought it was the right idea, and I did too—at the time."

And because you didn't know what you were doing, Sarah thought.

"And because I didn't know what in the hell I was doing," Max said. Sarah smiled a little.

"Elizabeth and I are in love," Max went on, his voice sounding more strained by the second. He was *scared,* Sarah realized, of *her* opinion of *him!*

Gratified by her newfound power, Sarah made Max sweat for a second. "So why haven't you called off the wedding?" she asked.

Max looked even more scared and shrunken. *Now he's going to give me some earlspeak,* she thought wearily, *about family and duty and honor and all that crap.*

But instead Max's eyes shifted. "The situation with Lavinia is . . . complicated," he said.

Sarah wasn't about to give up the wedge she'd finally made in her communications with her dearest brother. "Complicated how?" she said, shifting slightly to make room for the waitress to put down their plates of spinach pie.

Max stuck in his fork and began chewing vigorously. "Why don't we eat a bit?" he suggested.

Sarah rolled her eyes. She knew that gambit well.

When the waitress had finally cleared away their plates, Sarah gave Max a nod to continue. "So . . . ," she said.

"So," Max said.

Sarah sighed—honestly, her brother could be incredibly annoying. "So what's the situation with Lavinia?" she demanded again.

By this time, Sarah was sure, Max had had time to formulate a sufficiently cloaked response to her question. She was not disappointed.

"Lavinia has presented . . . certain issues that make it difficult to suspend the wedding right now."

Sarah felt a lightbulb flick on in her head. There was another way to figure out what Max wasn't telling her, and it wasn't to inject Max with truth serum and wait for him to spill.

"I understand," Sarah said, sitting up and drumming her fingers on the table. "I should probably get back to school."

Max looked at her suspiciously. "Sure you don't want some tea or anything?" he asked.

"Nope," Sarah said, now jiggling her knee

under the table rapidly. Max put his hand out to stop her. "You're not mad or anything?" he asked.

"Nope," Sarah said, rattling the words off as if from a cue card. "I-really-appreciate-your-speaking-to-me-and-now-I-understand-everything."

Out on the street, Max clapped his hand on her shoulder. "Sure you're okay?" he said worriedly.

But Sarah was already consumed with mental preparations for her plan. "Absolutely," she said, putting her hand over her brother's.

On Thursday morning Elizabeth received a rare gift from Mary at breakfast.

"You girls have been working so hard lately," she said, looking at Elizabeth particularly with concern. As usual, Vanessa was buried glumly in her bowl of porridge, and Alice had yet to arrive from the sleep that she coveted so dearly. Elizabeth had to fight the urge to look behind her to see if some other hard-working urchins had arrived in the Pennington kitchen—working hard? Them? She'd practically spent the entire week in her room, dealing with the psychodrama of her current circumstances.

"Why don't you take the morning off, Elizabeth," Mary said crisply, rinsing her plate in the sink and brushing her hands off briskly on her apron.

But I haven't been doing anything at all! Elizabeth wanted to cry. She looked at Vanessa, who raised her eyebrows and shrugged. *Don't say no to a morning off,* her expression seemed to say.

Slowly Elizabeth untied her apron and stood up. Mary had already disappeared up the steps. By the time Elizabeth reached her room upstairs to shower and change into street clothes, she'd reassured herself that no one would be chasing her down to tell her it had all been a mistake.

Maybe Mary's trying to make up for last Monday with Lavinia, Elizabeth thought as the tube rattled its way into Notting Hill. A warm blush spread through her—the spirit of Christmas was everywhere.

Lavinia Worm Thurston notwithstanding, Elizabeth added sourly.

Elizabeth spent the morning ducking in and out of what seemed like hundreds of colorful shops. She found a gray silk scarf with delicate beadwork in a Thai stand rippling with skirts and richly woven belts that was perfect for Vanessa, then a small leather journal for Alice, who had often admired Elizabeth's ordinary spiral notebooks. Mary was easily taken care of with a deep box of two-inch truffles and Cook with a sea green bowl filled with delicious soaps.

That would be perfect for Max, Elizabeth found herself thinking frequently, fingering silk ties and strange leather vests and sets of bronze cuff links.

Finally, in an old bookshop, she came across a first edition of J. D. Salinger's *Nine Stories*. She allowed herself to splurge, knowing that if Max hadn't read "A Perfect Day for Bananafish" yet, it was time.

I can buy him a good-bye gift, Elizabeth thought stubbornly, fighting the voices that told her to save her money for her plane ticket home. *After all, the only thing I've ever given him is free advice on how to use the editing function on his computer.*

And my virginity, Elizabeth added after a second, catching a glimpse of her rueful expression in the store's window. She burst into giggles at her unmitigated dopiness.

Buying presents for her family—a task she had usually started around July—was much harder. As she walked around, she couldn't help thinking how much Jessica would like that basket purse, those sky blue sling-back heels, that black beaded flapper helmet. She was particularly taken by a bloodred sake service in a Japanese tea shop and only darted away when the salesgirl, smiling, approached and asked if she would like to see anything in particular.

Walking back onto the busy street, choked with shoppers, Elizabeth tried to calm her breathing. *So you won't get gifts for your family this year,* she tried to tell herself, thinking both how easy and how hard it would be to buy the red china for Jessica or the matching bamboo blinds she knew her parents would love. *It's a funny year.*

Funny. The thought of not buying gifts for her family for Christmas made her sick to her stomach.

Elizabeth ducked into a café to have a cup of coffee—*no more tea!* her American side sang happily—and to gather herself. As she finally settled her purchases around her legs, she noticed that computer terminals lined the back wall of the café. She'd emailed Nina last month, then had felt a bit funny about it and hadn't emailed her old friend since. Perhaps it was time to make contact again.

The computers beckoned her.

Maybe she'll say something about your family.

Or Jessica.

Something.

Elizabeth moved all her stuff to a terminal and typed in Nina's email address. She quickly wrote her a message that said she was sorry she'd been so AWOL, that she couldn't apologize enough for it

And then she waited, hoping that Nina was online at this exact moment, despite the time difference, checking out websites or emailing friends.

Friends. *Nina Harper was my best friend at one time*, Elizabeth thought. *And now, we barely know anything about each other's lives.*

A reply pinged on the screen. Elizabeth sat bolt upright.

Elizabeth, the email from Nina read.

I'm not even going to scream at you for disappearing again after making contact last month. Okay, maybe a little. I swear I was about to send a search party out to Buckingham Palace for you.

Elizabeth laughed and scrolled down.

On a more serious note, your family is totally freaking out. Your sister especially. They told me if I heard from you to tell you they love you, they miss you, and they want you to come home.

Elizabeth felt an odd spinning sensation in her head. So she hadn't been disowned! *They* missed *her!* And they wanted her back!

Also, girl, you know Sweet Valley's not the same with you away. Remember Chloe Murphy, that little sophomore who was always borrowing my miniskirts? Well, she's got a steady boyfriend now, and he looks gooooood. I, on the other hand, have been hitting the books, and I have nothing but straight A's to show for my semester—which, to tell you the truth, is good enough for me.

Elizabeth found herself blinking back tears. It was amazing—it was like she could almost *hear* Nina's voice zinging across cyberspace.

And you'll never guess who else got straight A's! (Well, one B, but who's counting?) None other than your formerly "underperforming" sister, Jessica.

Elizabeth sat back. That *was* a shocker. But what did it mean?

Well, for one, that she's not spending all day with Sam and his Playstation, Elizabeth thought, remembering her former boyfriend's favorite vice. *Unless he's started to hit the books too.*

That thought did make Elizabeth laugh.

So anyway, what else can I say but get yourself home as soon as possible! And don't you dare ever leave us for people who fry everything again!

That sentence was followed by a row of *x*'s and *o*'s, Nina's typical sign-off. Except this time there was a *love* at the end.

Elizabeth sat back in the chair, her head swimming. From the corner speakers Bananarama's version of "Little Soldier Boy" came screaming over the sound system.

Was it time to go home?

As usual, Sarah went over every element of her plan with Victoria.

It was simple, she explained as they walked through the halls, each clutching a stack of textbooks. Max and Elizabeth must talk sometime, right? Especially at a moment of high stress like this. And even if they didn't, Elizabeth was sure to spill some juicy tidbits to her coworkers, Alice and Vanessa. Something that would help Sarah help Max get out of marrying Lavinia.

She'd simply leave dinner early, duck up into

the closet of the servants' room, and wait for the info to buzz out over the wires.

As Sarah slipped an extra chocolate scone into her purse at lunch—"for surveillance rations," she explained—Victoria had only one question.

"What about Bones?" she asked.

Sarah frowned. She hadn't thought about Bones at all since that terrible night in the pub, she realized.

"I guess Bones is okay," she finally said. "I just want to work out all this stuff with my brother first, that's all."

Victoria's mouth hung agape. "God," she finally said, shutting it. "You must *really* love your brother."

I do, Sarah realized, cramming an apricot scone into her mouth for strength before it was time for biology. *And I'm not going to let him screw up his life if I can help it.*

That night at dinner everything went perfectly. Pleading an upset stomach, Sarah disappeared upstairs after the soup course, which she was certain would be enough to satisfy her, what with the scones and jelly worms she had crammed in her purse. She wouldn't be up there for hours, after all, would she?

She hoped not.

Darting across to the back stairway, Sarah climbed

up the narrow steps and walked to the door at the end of the hall. Jiggling the knob to make sure it was unlocked, she threw open the door in one motion.

If anyone's here, Sarah thought, *I'll just say that I heard some strange noises and I came up to check that everything was okay.*

The room was perfectly empty.

Sarah gazed across the profoundly unvast expanse, taking in the three narrow cots and the rickety bureaus. *Jeez,* she thought, making a mental note to tell the earl to get some better furniture for his workers. *I'm glad I'm not a maid in this house.*

Checking the closet to make sure that it was large enough to accommodate her for what might be quite a sit-in, she settled herself down and closed the door all but a crack.

Don't fall asleep, she warned herself, feeling the dark, enclosed space already sending her off to dreamland.

Don't worry, a calmer part of her responded. *They'll wake you up when they get back.*

With their talking.

After they finished serving dinner, Elizabeth and Alice both showered and tried to convince Vanessa to do the same.

"It's an Audrey Hepburn festival!" Alice cried. "How can you not come?"

Vanessa lay on her bed, trying not to stare at the clock. James was coming—she knew—at seven, and it was six-fifteen. Were they ever going to leave?

"Just like this," Vanessa said, and snapped her fingers.

All day she had been thinking about her date with James, alternately getting dreamy and panicking. *I hope he's not thinking of going to see* Breakfast at Tiffany's, she thought once she realized where Elizabeth and Alice were going. *That's not exactly how I want to break the news to everyone.*

Not that they would even notice, Vanessa thought. Elizabeth had been walking around for a day or two looking incredibly calm—preternaturally calm, Vanessa thought, for a girl in her situation. And Alice, as usual, was off down her own rabbit hole.

Part of Vanessa's nervousness came from the fact that she had made a difficult decision. She had decided to tell James right away about her situation with the earl. Then, if he didn't want to get involved in a bloody family feud, there would be no hard feelings.

And I won't be living a lie with him right from the start, Vanessa thought, feeling freer than she had in years.

At six-thirty Elizabeth and Alice—*Finally,* Vanessa exhaled—left. Snatching another quick look at the clock, Vanessa bolted for the shower. By six fifty-three she was fully showered, dressed, and perfumed, her hair leaving a damp circle on the back of her collar.

At six fifty-eight, there was a knock on her door.

With my luck, that'll be Mary, Vanessa thought, smoothing down her long, black skirt. Steeling herself, Vanessa opened the door.

There stood James, a full bouquet of fire lilies in his left hand, looking like he'd been as scared that there would be nobody behind the door as she had been that the wrong person would be knocking. His face lit up immediately. Dropping the flowers to his side, James immediately swept Vanessa into a deep, long kiss.

"These are beautiful," Vanessa finally said, disengaging herself slightly and taking the flowers from James's hand.

"Oh, these? These aren't for you. These are for Mary," James deadpanned. "Sorry for any confusion."

Vanessa smirked and went to fill an old glass jar with water, dumping out the handful of pence and pens it had been holding. Returning to the room, she plunked the flowers in it and stood back to admire the array.

"I'm amazed that you knew I liked orange flowers," Vanessa said.

Now it was James's turn to smirk. "They're sparky. Like you," he offered.

As usual, Vanessa was enjoying their badinage, but she wanted to get the difficult part out of the way first so they could enjoy the rest of the date. "James, I've got something to tell you," she said, sitting opposite him on Elizabeth's bed.

"Don't tell me," James said, holding a hand up. "You're lactose intolerant?"

Vanessa laughed, then tried to look serious. "James, it's a real thing," she said, trying to keep the pleading tone out of her voice. "So let me just get it out, and then you can tell me what you think about it."

James immediately assumed a more proper expression. "All right," he said, his voice filled with real—Vanessa could tell—concern.

She couldn't look at him, though—not while she was telling it. "It's a long story," she began.

James smiled and touched her knee briefly. "Don't worry," he said. "I've been getting quite a few of those lately."

From your students, about late papers, she thought suddenly, then stopped herself. She had to stop making so much of the class difference between herself and James, or she would ruin everything.

"Good," she said, trying to keep her voice from trembling. "Actually, it's not long at all—it's just a little strange."

James was silent for a moment. "That's okay," he finally said.

"I'm not working in this house because I need the money," Vanessa said, hoping James wouldn't cut her off with some joke about her being an heiress. "I'm working in this house," she said, "because the earl is my father."

Although she wasn't looking at him directly, she could hear that James was standing up slowly. She forced herself to look up, directly into his face, hoping that he wasn't too freaked out.

"The earl caused my mother's death," Vanessa continued, her voice breaking.

James's face was like a death mask. He looked down at her, and Vanessa could feel the fury coming off him like waves of heat.

"So you're the one," he finally said, looking down at her like he wanted to stamp her out of existence with the sole of his shoe.

Vanessa was flabbergasted. Had James known, then? Had the entire family known the truth this entire time? And kept it from her?

"You're the one ruining Max's life," James continued, his voice sounding oddly flat, like the voice from a computer. "You sold Lavinia the information to blackmail the earl!"

Now Vanessa was completely lost—but she could read James's expression very well, and it wasn't good. It looked like one of her mother's boyfriends had looked right before he overturned the kitchen table onto her mother's lap.

"How much did she give you for it?" James asked, looking down at Vanessa with a terrible expression, his hands suddenly drawn into fists.

"James!" Vanessa said, feeling the tears running down her face and hating herself for her weakness. "I swear, I never—"

"Don't speak to me," James said, cutting her off. "You've got what you wanted, Vanessa—you're finally rid of me." He marched to the door to leave, then turned around for one parting shot. "Don't ever speak to me again," he spat, then slammed the door behind him.

Vanessa couldn't speak. She bit her knuckles to stem the flow of tears.

It's over, she thought.

It was a great surprise to her when Sarah fell out of the closet, weeping hysterically.

Chapter
Ten

James couldn't believe he'd been so colossally stupid.

He was striding across Pennington House's grounds as fast as he could go, taking such big strides that he was halfway to the road before he realized where he was. He couldn't, he realized, remember anything—how he'd gotten downstairs, whether he had his coat, what his last name was— since he'd slammed the door in Vanessa's face.

Vanessa's beautiful face.

My parents were right, he thought. *She really is just money—money—money-chasing rubbish!*

Suddenly James found himself in the middle of an open glade, pine trees surrounding a bed of pine needles, snow, and dirt. He had absolutely no idea where he was, he realized.

With a thump James sat down on the ground and put his head in his hands. *It figures,* he thought bitterly. *The minute I land the girl of my dreams, I realize she's not the girl of my dreams at all.*

Like a howling dog, James twisted his head up to find the moon. It was there in its regular place, its half belly gazing down at him beneficently.

How had it happened? James wondered. Had Vanessa simply approached Lavinia innocently after some brunch or cocktail party and thrust the packet of damning evidence in her hand? Had she quoted the price aloud or written it on a slip of paper?

Suddenly James remembered Max. "Damn," he groaned aloud, raking his hands through the snowy dirt. *This means that everything Max is afraid of is true,* he thought, feeling a terrible sinking sensation. The earl was like a father to him enough that he felt shamed and appalled too.

James groaned again, then groaned louder. "Damn," he said, letting the wind carry the words away. *"Damn!"*

That act in the bedroom, James thought. *All that crying, that look of surprise. How precious.* He ground his teeth, wondering how he'd allowed himself to be taken in by all of Vanessa's manipulations.

Except it hadn't seemed like an act at all, James suddenly realized.

James turned the snow over more slowly in his hands, barely feeling the icy crystals against his skin. Was Vanessa really that good an actress? he wondered.

If she could help Lavinia to blackmail Max, she could do anything, James thought. Except he didn't know if Vanessa really had helped Lavinia blackmail Max.

Christ, man, if she's telling the truth, then you've done what she's already always afraid you're going to do—jumped to the absolute worst conclusion about her, no questions asked.

James let a handful of snow drift through his fingers.

How would Vanessa know that Lavinia needed something to blackmail Max with anyway? James wondered. *Especially when Elizabeth is her friend. It's not like Lavinia's marching around asking, Who's the earl's illegitimate child because I need some proof to blackmail Max with!*

People know and do all sorts of things, his brain hissed insistently. *Look at the earl.* He put his hands flat down in the snow. For some reason, the words, "It's not like Lavinia's marching around . . . ," kept running through his head.

Suddenly James stood up. "Oh my God," he whispered.

What if Vanessa *hadn't* been acting? What if Lavinia had no idea who the earl's child was—she just knew he had one? Lavinia wouldn't need to know who the child was, after all. *She wouldn't need to know!*

What if the girls hadn't spoken more than ten words to each other in all of their natural lives, nine of which were, "Please," and, "Thank you"?

"This might really all just be a very unfortunate coincidence," James said aloud, his stomach twisting with what he might have just done.

Suddenly he found himself striding back toward the house. His walk became a run, and then his run became a flat-out gallop.

He had to find Vanessa and apologize. Right away.

Before he lost her forever.

Sarah had thought that seeing Max and Elizabeth holding hands was bad.

When the three girls had finally returned to the room, the slamming open of the door had woken Sarah immediately. The chocolate scone had tumbled to the floor, but other than that, she had made no sudden moves.

When it had seemed that Alice and Elizabeth were going to leave Vanessa to a leisurely evening at home, Sarah had cursed her bad luck. *I might,* she thought, *be spending the night on this empty closet floor.*

But when Vanessa suddenly left the room and Sarah heard a shower running, instead of dashing back downstairs to her comfy, well-stocked bed, she stayed exactly where she was.

Just sit tight, the voice in her head said, and she felt the back of her scalp prickle.

When there was a knock on the door, Sarah had to stop herself from cheering. *Something's going to happen now, I know it!* she thought. She wasn't even that surprised to hear James's voice booming about in the small room. After all, James mopped the floor with his tongue, practically, every time Vanessa entered the room.

But she was surprised to hear that Vanessa, evidently, felt something of the same way toward James. "These are beautiful," she heard Vanessa murmur, right after the unmistakable sound of them snogging. Sarah's eyes grew wide. This might not exactly be the piece of gossip she had come up here to find, but man, was she going to have some juicy tidbits for Victoria tomorrow!

When the conversation had suddenly taken a serious turn, Sarah had pricked up her ears. It wasn't that she was expecting to hear anything having to do with Max, Lavinia, or Elizabeth. But she hadn't lived in the same house with the cool, mysterious Vanessa for months without developing some interest in the girl. *Now,* Sarah thought, *I'm finally going to get some dirt!*

And dirt was exactly what she'd gotten.

Sitting on the bare, cold floor with the voices shouting around her, Sarah had had to make a supreme effort not to start shouting herself. She *couldn't,* absolutely *couldn't,* believe what she was hearing.

Lavinia was blackmailing Max?

Her father had another child?

Vanessa was—*her sister?*

Large, harsh gulps began to escape from her mouth, as if the closet had suddenly been drained of oxygen. James and Vanessa didn't hear her over their shouting. But she could still hear them—oh, she could hear them.

When the door slammed, Sarah had jumped to her feet. She had only one—one!—desire: to find her father and make him explain everything to her *right* away.

She staggered out of the closet.

She didn't expect to see Vanessa, weeping just as hysterically as she was, still in the room.

Vanessa looked at Sarah like she had suddenly descended from a spaceship.

Slowly, painfully, she got to her feet. "Sarah," she said, casting about for a moment before she could even remember the name of the girl she had served breakfast, lunch, and dinner to for the past year. The only question she could ask was the obvious: "What are you doing here?"

Sarah couldn't speak. She simply pointed, eerily, at the closed oak door. Then, like a rabbit, she dashed through it.

Vanessa didn't think; she simply acted. As if her shoes were spring-loaded, she dashed through the door in hot pursuit.

Think, Vanessa chastened herself, following the girl's flip of brown hair like the open door of a moving train. *Think, think, think, think, think.*

Vanessa could hear large, gasping sobs coming from somewhere. As Sarah rounded the corner of the front hall and began the long, careening path toward the earl's office, Vanessa realized they were her own.

The two girls nearly collided at the door, then smashed into the quiet of the earl's office like bombardiers. "Father!" Sarah screamed, shattering the extreme silence. The scream hung in the air for a moment, like smoke.

"What*ever* is—," the earl said, sitting upright in surprise. Then he saw Vanessa. "The matter . . ." He trailed off, looking from one weeping face to the other.

Vanessa finally found her voice. "I didn't tell her," she jabbered, knowing that she sounded hysterical but unable to stop herself. "She overheard us talking, that was all. She overheard a conversation."

Once, twice, the earl nodded. He put his pipe slowly down on the desk.

"Father," Sarah screamed again—a shrill, hunted sound. *"What is going on?"*

Then she put her face in her hands and began to sob.

The earl came around from behind the desk and put his arm around Sarah immediately, making what Vanessa realized were supposed to be soothing sounds, although they sounded more like the clucking of a chicken. "There, there," he said, patting Sarah briskly on the back. "We'll get this sorted out straightaway, don't you worry."

We will? Vanessa thought in surprise. Was this the time for the earl to spin some fairy tale so that the entire family—James included—could close ranks around her forever?

But even though the earl was patting Sarah's back, he was looking Vanessa in the eye. "I hoped to wait until the wedding was over to resolve this matter," he said, Vanessa's skin prickling at the words. *This matter!* she thought—couldn't he do better than that? "But clearly that will not be possible," the earl finished. He reached over to the intercom and hit the button. It crackled alive. "Yes, sir?" came Mary's voice feebly from the kitchen.

"Send Max down to my study immediately," the earl said, and released the button.

Mary's voice came back dry but clear. "Yes, sir," she said.

Vanessa couldn't believe it. The earl was going to tell the truth: to his family, to everyone.

She was going to be acknowledged.

As if he had been reading her mind, the earl spoke again: this time to both of them. "It's time for the truth to come out," he said, still stroking Sarah's hair through her snuffles. "Long past time, I think."

Something in Mary's tone made Max hop double-quick down to the earl's office.

Stop being stupid, Max, he told himself as he tripped down the stairs. *Dad's probably just wanting to have a last-cigar-with-the-bachelor kind of thing or something.*

It wasn't possible that he had heard about Lavinia and was confronting *Max,* was it?

When he opened the door and saw his white-faced father, white-faced sister, and white-faced Vanessa, he had no idea what was going on.

"Dad," he said, hoping that no tragedy—like when Sarah had tried to frame Elizabeth for destroying Lavinia's wedding dress—had occurred again. Or had Lavinia decided to have *Vanessa* fired for some reason? "If this has something to do with me and Lavinia, I want to tell you—"

The earl cut him off. "Sit down, Max," he said, giving Max the sudden chills. "I have something to tell all of you, and the sooner I do it, the sooner this whole mess will be resolved."

Max took a seat as quickly as he could. Good Lord, was it possible that his father had some *other* huge confession to make, one that involved Vanessa in some way? Or was his father actually going to confess to having an illegitimate child?

Then what was Vanessa doing here?

A strange prickling sensation rushed up the back of Max's head. He looked slowly from Vanessa's profile to the earl's, then at Sarah's. There it was—it was unmistakable. How could he have missed it all this time?

Instead of going back behind his desk, the earl remained standing, although he faced one of his rows of bookshelves instead of the three of them. He gave a long, shattering sigh.

"I thought I would allow this revelation to come out after the nuptials," the earl began, "so that it didn't overshadow the ceremony. That was wrong, I realize now. And since I've handled this situation so poorly, I should not be surprised that it has degenerated horribly."

The earl turned briefly to face all of them. His voice was tight. "For that, I apologize," he said flatly.

Max couldn't contain himself—he almost

groaned aloud. *Father, are you about to tell us,* he wanted to shout, *that you're Vanessa's father?*

Max glanced over at his sister, whose face was puffy and red with crying. He had a sudden urge to cover her ears—to protect her from whatever she was about to hear.

Vanessa was looking at the earl as if her own skin would shatter if she took her glance away from him for a minute. Her eyes shone, and her face had a terrible, fevered glow. She looked just like Max felt—like she wanted to duck from a blow she knew was about to come.

But what the earl said next was not what Max expected at all.

"You remember your uncle Giles," the earl tossed out at Max and Sarah.

Sarah's face remained unmoved. Max shifted in his seat.

"Yes, Father," Max said, as politely as he could, under the circumstances. "The brother you had, who died—"

"He didn't die," the earl said, his head looking at the lowest shelf of his bookcases.

Max wanted to shake him. "No?" he asked, the question popping out of his mouth like a marble that rolled around a while on the floor before it came to a stop.

"He didn't die," the earl repeated. "He's alive

right now, in the States. California, in fact."

Max couldn't speak. This was interesting, of course, but what did it have to do with anything?

"Vanessa," the earl said, finally turning and looking them all in the eye. "Giles is my twin brother. That man is your father. I did not have an affair with anyone. My brother, older by two minutes, held the title of earl, and you simply didn't know that, so you assumed I was the earl your mother had written of in her letters."

Suddenly they were all jabbering at once. "Why didn't you tell me this before?" Vanessa demanded.

"Lavinia's wrong!" Max shouted.

"You don't have a mistress?" Sarah shrieked.

The earl held up his hand, then rubbed it slowly on his forehead. "Please," he said wearily. "This secret has—lain so long in this family. Just give me a little time to explain."

Max quieted down, but he couldn't quiet down the sudden thrill in his heart. Lavinia had nothing—*nothing*—on him or on his family!

Could it possibly be?

I shouldn't have waited, Max thought suddenly. *I shouldn't have done this to Elizabeth. I was a terrible coward. I should have trusted in my father.*

And in myself.

Vanessa had risen up out of her seat, but now she sat again, her eyes burning. "Why didn't you tell me about my father right away?" she shouted again, then burst into noisy tears.

Max could have sworn that the earl's eyes misted a little too. He walked over to Vanessa and put his hand on her knee, kneeling slightly with effort. "My dear," he said gently. "I'm a stupid man. A stupid old man who didn't know how to let the skeletons out of the closet."

Vanessa continued to cry, inconsolable. Sarah watched her with fascination, as if she'd never seen anything like it before. Even Max was amazed. *So Vanessa does have feelings!* he thought, thinking of how, in all the time he'd known her, he'd only seen the same stiff, formal mask.

Well. Like uncle, like niece, Max thought, watching with the same amazement as the earl's face cracked and ran.

"Your father was very much in love with your mother, my dear," the earl continued, tears running down the dry paper of his face freely now. "He wanted to marry her more than anything in the world. He—and I—had no idea you even existed."

Vanessa stopped crying a little bit and peeked up at the earl. "He did want to marry her?" she breathed.

"Yes, he did," the earl continued, more eagerly now that Vanessa seemed to be quieting down. "They were quite the romance," he said, almost chuckling.

This is absolutely unbelievable, Max thought, looking from Vanessa's face to the earl's and back again. *Is this the same man who was always sending Elizabeth away with a "That will be all"?*

Vanessa had stopped crying and took the earl's hand in her own, gripping it like she was holding on for dear life. "What happened?" she whispered.

The earl's face suddenly looked terribly old. "My father," he said. "My father wouldn't have it."

Max tried to remember his grandfather. All he could get was a cloudy image of long legs enclosed in worsted wool and an extremely, almost frighteningly, erect carriage.

"So why didn't he just take her with him to California?" Vanessa asked. "Why couldn't he have taken us with him?" she said, beginning to sob again.

The earl's face fell. "My father," he said, "told Giles that if he so much as looked at your mother one more time, he would make sure that Giles never, ever saw her again."

The room was silent while that information sank in. Sarah began to weep—fretful, frightened tears. Max gasped. Vanessa looked wooden, then stony, then beaten.

"Does he know about me?" Vanessa finally asked.

The earl stroked Vanessa's knee. "I don't know," he finally admitted. "I haven't spoken to him in almost nineteen years."

Chapter
Eleven

Suddenly, in the midst of the most interesting twenty minutes of Vanessa's life, Max spoke up and made them a little more interesting.

"Lavinia knows," he said.

The room suddenly exploded again, although this time it was the earl and Vanessa who were amazed. "What do you mean, Lavinia knows?" she asked while the earl said, "Lavinia knows about Giles and Vanessa?"

Vanessa's mind was racing. *Could my father have known about me all these years and not made any effort to get me?* Vanessa thought. Her spirits, which had risen precipitously in the past moments, fell again.

"I mean, she doesn't k-know it's *you*, Vanessa," Max stammered, looking red and uncomfortable with the new intimacy implied in his just assumed role of first cousin. "But she knows that there was a child somewhere."

The earl fastened his gaze on Max. "And she told you this, Max?" he asked sharply.

Max looked like he wanted to disappear into the floor. "She said it was you, Dad," he finally murmured. "She claims her mother told her as leverage before she died."

Vanessa wanted to laugh out loud. So she wasn't the only one with that delusion!

The earl looked at Vanessa, then at Max. "Well, perhaps her mother wanted to keep the secret in her own way by naming me as the one who'd had an affair, yet give Lavinia *something* to use in the event she'd need to hold something over the family. Something that wouldn't totally hold up as true. Why didn't you tell me, Max?" he finally asked. "Did you think we couldn't talk about it?"

Now Max looked like he was the one who wanted to laugh. "Well, er, it's not that simple, Dad," he finally said, and his tone grew serious. "Lavinia threatened to tell the papers and cause a scandal if I didn't marry her."

Now, the earl—*Uncle Pennington,* Vanessa corrected—looked like he had been shot in the knees. "Oh, she did?" he asked, his voice betraying just a bit of a tremor. "I wasn't aware that you didn't want to marry Lavinia," he said to Max.

Max looked his father squarely in the eye. "It seems there's lots of things we should have been discussing," he said boldly.

Ouch, Vanessa thought, looking at how the blow positively crumpled the earl. He leaned back and took a seat, taking his handkerchief out of his pocket and dabbing it over his forehead.

"I guess I deserved that, my boy," the earl said, looking from Max to Vanessa to Sarah and back down at his hands. "You all have a perfect right to be angry with me."

Vanessa wilted. The earl wasn't the terrible monster she had thought; he was just a nice man, propped up by some very silly concepts. Suddenly she found herself across the room. "I forgive you," she said, taking his hand.

The earl looked up. "You do?" he asked, then pulled her to him in a hug.

Finally, from across the room, Sarah spoke up. "I hate to break up this little family moment, Dads," she said, "but are you still going to make Max marry Lavinia?"

The earl pulled back from the embrace and blew his nose energetically. "From now on and heretofore," he began in the sonorous tone he used to speak to Parliament, "in the Pennington family, anyone can marry whomever they want." He patted the side of the chair next to him and motioned for

Sarah to come over. When she did, he put his other arm around her, drawing both Sarah and Vanessa close. He looked over at Max with glittering, proud eyes. "Max, my boy, you know what you're about. I'm staying out of it," he declared, and planted a kiss on both Sarah and Vanessa's cheeks.

Max bounded up the stairs to the servants' quarters like he was in a no-gravity environment.

Damn, he suddenly realized, *I don't have any flowers and chocolates or anything.*

Or a ring, he added after a moment.

As he neared Elizabeth's door, Max looked for the telltale streak of light under the door. There was none. He decided to knock gently. "Elizabeth?" he said softly, hoping that he wasn't going to be waking up the whole floor.

He leaned in to the door to hear if anyone was moving around inside. It didn't seem like anyone was. His heart pounding, Max slowly turned the knob and opened the door onto the darkened room.

It was completely empty.

"Damn!" Max said, aloud this time. Where could she be? He wanted to resolve everything now—before something else happened and she somehow slipped through his fingers.

He could leave a note, couldn't he? Max searched his pockets for a scrap of paper. Shoot. Nothing.

Suddenly an idea struck him. He walked back downstairs. There *was* something he could give Elizabeth, he realized.

Flooded with intensity of purpose, Max whipped out the cell phone Lavinia had given him, ignoring the full-mailbox icon that indicated she had left him six thousand messages since Tuesday. "Operator," he said, after getting the company on the line. "I need to find a person in Sweet Valley, California."

As the operator ran through gigabytes of information with much whirring and clicking, Max reached behind his back and silently crossed his fingers. *Now, you be home, all right?* he urged a girl he had never met before.

As the phone rang, Max realized he was actually bouncing on the balls of his feet with anxiety. Smiling, he lowered himself down, all the while thinking, *Pick up, pick up, pick up,* like some skipping CD.

And just like that, someone did. "Hello?" a girl said, sounding both chipper and irritated at the same time.

She also sounded eerily like Elizabeth.

Max swallowed. "Jessica Wakefield?"

"Yes," came the voice. "You're interrupting my sunbathing during the last sun rays of the afternoon, so this had better be good, whoever you are."

"Uh, I'm sorry to call so suddenly," he began, reminding himself not to give Jessica anything like the scare he had given Sarah yesterday. "First of all, don't be alarmed. Nothing is wrong. But my name is Max Pennington, and I'm calling from England. It's about your sister."

Vanessa found James exactly where she'd hoped he'd be: wandering across the lawn like Hamlet's ghost.

"James!" she cried, speeding up in his direction, hoping that he was waiting for her.

Thankfully, James didn't turn away and run. Instead he reacted as if he had been looking for her for hours. "Vanessa!" James shouted across the lawn. "I'm sorry! I'm sorry!"

"No, I'm sorry," Vanessa began to shout back, laughing and crying at the same time. They met in the middle of the yard and clapped their arms around each other like old war buddies.

After Vanessa had told the earl that she planned to go to California right away to seek out her father, the earl had urged her to stay through the holidays, and Sarah—her new cousin!—had seconded the motion eagerly. "I'll have to see," Vanessa said, feeling the new bliss of a real family like a warm room after hours in the cold.

Then she remembered her fight with James.

"What is it?" the earl had said as Vanessa suddenly rose to her feet.

"I've got to find someone right away," she said, the words spilling out one after another. "And explain something."

"But who?" the earl asked. He looked at Sarah. "Will someone tell me what's going on?"

Sarah was reclining on the chair like a teenage czarina. She hit the earl lightly on the arm with the flat of her hand. "Oh, mind your business, Dads," she said, giving Vanessa a wicked smile. "Just because she's part of the family doesn't mean Vanessa doesn't have the right to a life of her own, does it?"

Why, the brat has a good side! Vanessa thought in astonishment. She smiled back—a real smile.

"Quite so," said the earl, tapping his pipe thoughtfully against his knee. "Quite so, quite so."

So Vanessa had run immediately out to the front hall to check if James's car was still in the driveway. Instead she saw James himself, tearing up the drive like a madman.

"I'm so glad you're still here," Vanessa said, responding to James's eager kisses with a few of her own.

James suddenly pushed her back and looked at her, his eyes urgent and worried. "Vanessa, you know I don't think anything bad about you, don't you?" he asked, and Vanessa nodded happily. "I'm so sorry—I'm just an ass. It's just that Max told me about Lavinia only recently, and I immediately thought—"

Vanessa put her fingers over his lips. "It's all right," she said. "I understand."

The astonishing thing was, she did. *I knew that James would still be here,* she thought, *even though he told me he never wanted to see me again. I knew he would realize his mistake. And do you know what that means?* she thought triumphantly.

I trust him.

"I did want to expose the earl," Vanessa told James. "Or at least, that's what I told myself. But now I know that I was staying on here for a different reason."

"What?" James asked, breathless.

"You," Vanessa said, closing him off from all response with another kiss.

"Max and the earl are causing a lot of trouble around here with their secrets," she finally grumbled through their locked lips.

"Um-hmm," James said, pulling back with a smack. "They certainly are."

Oh my God, Vanessa realized. *I haven't told him what the earl told me!*

"James—I have a long story to tell you," Vanessa said, giving him a light punch on the arm.

James grabbed her hand. "Tell it to me on the way to my house," he said. "I want to introduce you to my mum and dad as the girl I love."

Chapter
Twelve

On Friday morning Sarah walked out of Ms. Richards's class, clutching her books close to her chest. *It's a wonder I'm not bumping into walls and people,* she thought, still amazed at everything that had come to light in her family.

Suddenly she felt a hand on her arm. She turned around. It was Bones, looking unnaturally subdued in a pair of slick black cords and a gray sweater.

"Hey," Bones said, clutching her elbow.

"Hey," Sarah said. She realized with surprise that for the first time, she was looking Bones right in the face, but her brain wasn't buzzing with a thousand schemes to get him to flirt back with her.

Bones leaned against the wall and looked at her quizzically, shaking his head. "We've been a little worried about you, you know," he said, giving her elbow a playful shake, then crossing his arms and smiling.

Sarah tried to smile back, but she barely had the energy. "You and Victoria?" she asked.

Bones nodded, then jerked his head toward the classroom Sarah had just left. "And Ms. Richards too, actually," he added, then dropped his voice to a whisper. "But you didn't hear it from me."

Sarah suddenly felt the dull thudding of gladness. So, the world didn't really stop turning when she ducked out for a while—but it did note her absence.

"A lot of family stuff has been happening," Sarah tried to explain.

Bones raised an eyebrow. "Such as?" he asked.

Sarah glanced around them—students were starting to filter in for the next period's classes. She sighed.

"Well, for one, Max is definitely *not* going to marry the ice sculpture on Sunday," she began, using their favorite nickname for Lavinia.

Bones's eyes lit up. "Cool!" he said. "We can have a huge house party!"

Sarah felt a flicker of interest. That wasn't such a bad idea, actually. Would the kinder, gentler earl think so too? She decided to run the idea past him. She certainly didn't relish the prospect of calling up thousands of guests with Mary to tell them it was all off.

Bones was about to speak, but Sarah interrupted him. "Well, I should probably get to class," she said, nodding toward the biology room.

"Okay," Bones said. He looked crestfallen.

Sarah started to walk away, but something stopped her. *The truth must dazzle gradually.* Well, there had certainly been enough "gradually" between her and Bones, hadn't there? She turned back around.

"Bones," she said. He was standing at the locker, looking down at his shoes, but his head jerked up happily when she said his name.

"Yeah?" he asked.

Sarah felt the supreme confidence of not having it in her to beat around the bush anymore. "Why haven't you ever kissed me?" she demanded, not even caring if anyone overheard.

Bones's eyes lit up. "Do you think I should?" he asked.

Sarah gave a vehement nod—then bit her lip. "Duh," she said.

Bones reached forward and placed his lips on hers: softly, then stronger.

"Whoo-hoo!" a passing group of students yelled.

Slowly Sarah and Bones pulled apart. They

smiled at each other, suddenly shy. Sarah broke the silence with another question.

"Why haven't you done that *before?*" she asked, not even bothering to hide her irritation.

Bones smiled and shrugged. "Sarah, I'm crazy about you," he said. "It's just—I have girls throwing themselves at me all the time." His voice became lower. "But since the minute I met you, I knew you were special. So I relished the opportunity to . . . take it slow."

"Really?" Sarah asked.

"Is that all right?" Bones asked, reaching for her hand.

Sarah exhaled—for the first time in weeks, it felt like. She swung their hands between them like a jump rope. "It's more than all right," she said happily, pulling him down the hall with her. "At this point I'd say it was positively *brilliant.*"

By ten o'clock on Friday morning Max had searched what felt like every inch of Pennington House for Elizabeth. He'd gone up to her room before breakfast, but all he'd found was a sleepy Alice. "I don't know where either of them are." Alice yawned, gesturing to the empty, still made beds. "But I know Lizzie came home with me last night!" she called after Max, who had already rushed off to see if she was down in the kitchen with Mary.

Please, please, don't have run off to California,
Max repeated to himself, jogging around the
perimeter of the garden, fruitlessly looking for a
glimpse of a red hat and red mittens amidst the
newly fallen snow.

He had put step one of his plan into effect far
too easily, he now saw. And with Elizabeth missing, he was going to have an extremely hard time
bringing step two to the triumphant close he had
envisioned.

Suddenly Max remembered that he hadn't spoken to Lavinia yet. *Now, that's a loose end you should
be sure to tie up before Elizabeth gets back from wherever she is,* Max thought, jogging toward his car.

On the way out of the garden, he stopped and
chucked the cell phone into a mess of shrubbery.

She's got to be home, right? Max thought as he
pulled up Lavinia's huge, elegant drive. *What
could a girl possibly need to buy two days before her
wedding?*

Well, in Lavinia's case, a different groom, Max
realized, smiling.

The butler informed him that Lavinia was upstairs, "With Miss Rima." Rima Shushanskaya was
the eccentric Russian seamstress Lavinia had
turned to in hysteria after Sarah ripped the first
wedding veil to shreds.

This must be what's called the "final fitting,"

Max thought, unable to deny himself one last terrible pun. *Well, it's final, all right—which is fitting.*

"Lavinia?" Max asked, knocking on the door.

"We're in here!" Lavinia called, sounding like she was encased in a full-body cast.

Which wasn't far from the truth. From where Rima knelt at her feet, her mouth full of pins, Lavinia rose to the ceiling in a huge, enormous column of white.

"Well, it's about time you showed up," Lavinia said grumpily. "I was beginning to think you'd skipped the country."

Rima looked up, caught some current flowing from Lavinia to Max, then quickly removed the pins from her mouth. "I take coffee break," she said.

Max crossed his arms. This was the moment he had been waiting for now for months. He hoped that Rima hadn't left any sharp scissors in easy reach.

"Lavinia, you're not going to like what I have to say. But you're going to listen anyway," Max began.

Elizabeth and Alice were really worried about Vanessa. After a stolen hour or two reading the earl's old paperback edition of *Great Expectations* in a deliberately secluded nook in the library,

Elizabeth returned to the kitchen to find Alice nearly in tears.

"It's Vanessa," Alice confided softly across the table, her eyes wide with fear. "She didn't come home last night, and I can't find her *anywhere*."

Elizabeth glanced at the broad backs of Cook and Mary. "Does anyone else know?" she whispered.

"No," Alice said, keeping her eyes locked on the cup of tea in front of her. "I keep telling Mary she's upstairs doing a final check on all of the bathrooms. But she's going to catch on eventually."

At that exact moment the bell rang, signaling a delivery, nearly startling Elizabeth and Alice out of their wits. "That'll be the champagne!" Mary barked. She nodded toward the upstairs. "Elizabeth. Alice. Look smart."

"Let's just hope it's not Vanessa in a police car," Alice whispered as they walked quickly upstairs.

"Or a tank," Elizabeth added nervously, feeling a strange thrill of fear.

When Elizabeth swung open the door, her first thought was that she was losing her mind. Instead of a champagne deliveryman, there stood Jessica Wakefield, wrapped in what looked like eighty wool scarves, stamping her feet briskly from the cold.

"Jessica?" Elizabeth asked, feeling like she had seen a ghost. For a moment no one moved, except Alice, who kept looking back and forth at Elizabeth and Jessica in wonder.

"There's another one of Elizabeth!" Alice breathed.

Elizabeth heard a car door slam. Max jogged into view, jiggling his car keys, a huge grin on his face. "Merry Christmas," he said, beaming. "Or should I say, surprise?"

Suddenly Jessica practically knocked Elizabeth backward with a massive bear hug. "Oh, Lizzie, I'm so sorry for everything!" she yelled into her ear, practically blowing out Elizabeth's eardrum. "It wasn't what you thought, I swear! I was just so stupid, and then I thought you were dead! We've been *looking* for you and *looking* for you everywhere," she babbled, suddenly bursting into a fresh round of sobs.

Slowly Elizabeth felt her own cheeks get wet. She licked a tear that was dripping into her mouth.

"But how did you—" Elizabeth tried to say. She seemed to have lost the ability to form whole sentences. She just wanted to keep looking at her sister, who, stamping the snow from her feet, seemed very, very real and solid, not a ghost at all.

"Um, that was my fault," Max said, looking slightly abashed. "I hope you don't mind."

Elizabeth turned to him, perplexed. *Mind?* "I don't know how I'm ever going to thank you," she whispered, closing her eyes and clutching Jessica to her in a fierce embrace. She never wanted to let her go.

"So I'm soaking up the last of the afternoon rays, working on my tan, as usual," Jessica started chattering again, "and this guy calls and tells me to get on the next plane to England, pronto. I swear, I was scared I was going to wind up somewhere on the auction block in some country I've never heard of!"

Max had taken Elizabeth's other hand. "I know how you could thank me," he said softly.

Suddenly more car doors slammed. Laughing and talking, Vanessa and James ran up, stopping when they saw the stunned crowd at the door.

"Let me guess," Vanessa said dryly, looking from Elizabeth to Jessica. "Another family reunion?"

Alice reached across to Vanessa and gave her a solid shaking, her round face dizzy with relief and anger. "Vanessa, where have you *been?*" she asked. "We've been *worried* about you!"

Vanessa looked sideways at James, and a deep blush spread across her face. "I was . . . meeting my boyfriend's parents," she gushed with a huge smile. "And we were at the travel agent, booking a trip to America. I'm going to find my father. James is going to help me!"

Then everyone was jabbering at once. Typically, Jessica's voice rose above the rest. "I don't know what's going on," she said. "But somebody better fill me in, fast!"

Max pulled Elizabeth aside. "I've made arrangements for you to go home with your sister whenever you want," he said. "I know you want to spend time with your family."

Elizabeth felt a lump in her throat. Things hadn't worked about between them, it was true, but Max had proved himself to be a loving friend—and he was there when she needed him.

And that should be enough, Elizabeth thought, her eyes filling with tears again.

"Elizabeth, get over here and introduce me to these crazy people!" Jessica was laughing. She had already intertwined arms with Vanessa, and she was jabbering away with Alice and Vanessa as if they were old friends. From the far archway the earl appeared.

"What," he asked loudly, "is the cause of this commotion?"

A silence fell, but Max broke it. "Just a moment," he declared, smiling at his father and holding Elizabeth's arm so that she couldn't move away. "I have a question for Elizabeth, but

I'd rather ask it in front of everyone."

Elizabeth heard a sharp intake of breath from everyone, including herself. *He's not,* she thought, *going to ask if there's any more bacon?*

Max pulled a tiny, velvet box from his pocket. He crooked it open to reveal an antique diamond, surrounded by lovely filigree. "Getting this back took some doing." Max grinned, then laughed. "But I managed it in the end."

"Oh, Max," Elizabeth nearly whispered, unable to believe what was happening. "You're not going to marry Lavinia?"

"No," he said simply. "I most certainly am not."

Elizabeth threw herself into his arms. "I'm so happy for you!"

Max gently pulled away from her and bent down on one knee, the ring gleaming.

Elizabeth's mouth dropped open. "Max, w-what are you doing?" she stammered.

"Asking you to marry me, of course," he said. "Will you?" he asked hoarsely, looking desperately serious.

Elizabeth couldn't speak. Suddenly she found her tongue. "I love you, Max. I do. But I need to go home. I need to sort out things with my family. I came to California to escape my family, and now I need to go back home to find out who it is I really am. I need to do that first, before I can commit myself to anything or anyone."

He nodded, then gave her a small smile, then pulled her into a hug, then gave her a real smile. "You're doing the right thing, Elizabeth Wakefield."

She hugged him back, then pulled away and looked into his eyes. "I love you, Maxwell Pennington. I always will."

"Just you remember that this ring will always be waiting for you, Elizabeth," he said, then kissed her gently on the forehead.

"Well," the earl announced, tears in his eyes, "we might as well make use of the wedding plans by having a huge Christmas party. What say you all to that?"

Everyone cheered. There was laughing and shrieking. At one point Elizabeth wasn't sure if she had hugged James and Vanessa six times or not at all. As the din raised itself, Mary and Cook came around to inspect the commotion, and Sarah arrived home from school with some very cute boy in tow, who she led around by the hand like a large dog. "Oh, Dad!" Elizabeth heard her shriek when the earl had explained what was happening. "I love you!"

Suddenly Max was at Elizabeth's side again, shaking hands with James. On her other side, Jessica was clutching her hand tightly and babbling with Cook. Max pulled Elizabeth to him to whisper in her ear. "Have a safe trip home," he said, kissing her earlobe.

Elizabeth kissed him back, then looked around at the faces of James, Vanessa, Alice, Mary, Cook, the earl, and Jessica. She was surrounded by people she loved. She had her sister on one side of her and the guy who'd brought them back together on the other. And now she was going home to see the rest of the people she loved—the ones she had left behind.

She was going home. Maybe she'd stay in Sweet Valley and register at SVU to finish college. Or maybe she'd come back to England to Max.

Whatever she did, Elizabeth knew she'd always have Sweet Valley and England in her heart. Both places had become home.

Elizabeth Wakefield had come full circle.

Check out the **all-new....**

Sweet Valley Web site—

www.sweetvalley.com

New Features

Cool Prizes

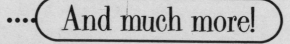

The ONLY official Web site!

Hot Links

And much more!